MW00626251

The Roaring Sands of Kandahar

The Roaring Sands of Kandahar

FARZANA EBRAHIMI

The Roaring Sands Of Kandahar
Copyright © 2021 Farzana Ebrihimi
All rights reserved.

No part of this book may be reproduced, stored in a retrieval system, or transmitted in any form or by any means—electronic, mechanical, photocopying, recording, or otherwise—without the prior written permission of the copyright holder. The only exception is by a reviewer, who may quote short excerpts in a review with appropriate citations.

Book cover design by Digital Content Creators
Book interior design by Digital Content Creators
Editing by Story Launcher

Farzana's books are available for order through Amazon.com

Twitter: @FarzanaEbrahimi
Instagram: roaringsandsof_kandahar
Facebook: Farzana Ebrahimi

First printing: October 2021
Published by Persona Publishing®
Story Launcher LLC: http://storylauncher.com

ISBN-13: 978-1-951451-09-7 (paper)
ISBN-13: ISBN: 978-1-951451-08-0 (Kindle)

Disclaimer: This is a work of historical fiction. All names and characters are either invented or used fictitiously. Any resemblance to real persons is coincidental.

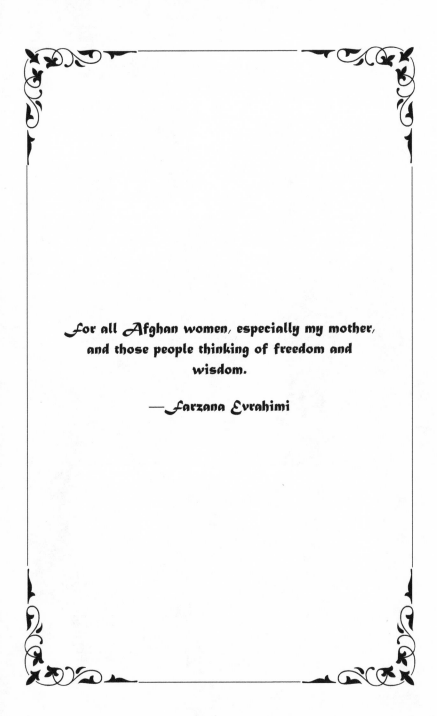

For all Afghan women, especially my mother, and those people thinking of freedom and wisdom.

—Farzana Evrahimi

Table of Contents

"Oh world, do you hear the voice of Afghan women? They are warriors who have been shouting for freedom in silence."

Farzana Ebrahimi

Chapter 1

Baba Wali

"Take one more step and I'll kill you."

Mina looked up through her burqa, startled. She had been distracted leaving the hillside mausoleum, her favorite place for Wednesday prayers, not watching where she stepped—thinking instead of the beauty of the silence and the smell of the yellow and white jasmine flowers bordering the tomb that brought a sweet, otherworldly feeling to her time there.

A tall man in a gray perahan tunban stood in front of her. He wore a dusty black vest over his traditional dress and a gun on his shoulder, which he pointed at Mina. "Are you blind? Can't you see it's harvest season?"

Mina struggled to focus her eyes; she felt dizzy. She blinked several times to adjust and then noticed where she stood. A pomegranate farm filled the left side of her vision—the blossoms had looked like beautiful flames from the mausoleum. The Arghandab River flowed to the right of her; she could tell by the line of trees following its path. Vineyards covered the surrounding hills in a carpet of yellow and green. The fresh perfume of the sea-buckthorn trees, which made every creature feel alive, mingled with the scent of the jasmine on the hillside. But she stood in the opium field at the bottom of the hill she had just left in peace, and something was stuck to her shoe.

"Give me your shoes," he commanded. She kicked them off quickly—simple black shoes, nothing to attract attention—yet somehow, they were still complicit in this predicament. The green seed pods shot skyward from the field, bursting with the milk of money, but some were already harvested and lay flat on the land, cracking and bursting with resin. He knelt in front of her and took a blade from his pocket. He carefully sliced the single opium pod from her shoe, his face looking as though he had just lost a child. He set his knife it in a small wooden box that he placed in his satchel, then looked at her from a face of wrinkled brown leather.

"If you had broken my neck with your step, I could more easily forgive you, but you broke a pod. What do I tell the owner now? He has counted each flower on this farm; he knows exactly how many afghani he will get for this harvest. I watch this land from sunrise to sunset to protect it from people like you."

Mina was still lightheaded from the pollen that filled her lungs. When the guard stood and turned to leave, she stepped quickly into her shoes and ran back up the green hill to the mausoleum. Once there, she entered the tomb and removed her scarf, pulling her long, black hair from where it stuck to the sweat of fear on her cheeks and tucked it behind her ears. She whispered a prayer and picked up a candle, holding its base in the melted candles next to the tomb until it could stay there without her hand.

Then, from a copper bowl at the corner of the tomb, she took a pinch of lucky rock salt and put it in her mouth, making the end of her tongue bitter. She knew she would eat all the salt in the bowl if it would help make her dream come true.

Slowly, other women came and ate the salt. Women with watery eyes waited for a miracle from a great man who had died hundreds of years earlier. Mina joined them to lean against the wall covered by the black smoke of the candles and closed her eyes. Waves of the candle's light danced in the air and the green cotton hugged the grave, transforming this tomb into a holy place. All the women who learned of this place came to rest their head on their lover's shoulder, the shoulder of the man called Baba Wali.

She was still whispering her prayers when the old wooden door of the tomb slowly opened. An older farmer man—another opium guard from the bottom of the hill—came inside. He rolled up his dusty, gray sleeves. With the corner of his turban, he cleaned his face. Then he stood by the grave and prayed. When he postulated, Mina noticed a deep crack in his heel that was filled with mud of the opium farm. When he finished his prayer, he looked at Mina from the corner of his eyes and smiled sadly. Then he touched his beard, fixed his turban, and left.

Afternoon arrived, and a strong wind shouted at the door, bringing back that unknown smell into the tomb again. The candles were slowly melting down, their smoke mixing with the taste of women's tears.

A strange, unexpected voice came from outside of the tomb, rough and deep. "Hey, old man, do you own this opium field?"

The old man replied, "No, I am only a gardener and a guard."

The rough voice asked, "Have you seen a woman here? She comes every Wednesday."

Mina's heart almost stopped. She knew this voice.

"Many women come every Wednesday; which one do you speak of?"

The rough voice shouted, "She's a young woman!"

The old man sighed. "Please let me finish my job now. You can go inside and look for yourself."

"You are a coward! Go inside and find her! Women do not hide their faces from you, old man! I can see nothing!" He paused and then growled, "If you do not find me that woman, I will drive my car through your opium field. You will be killed, and your grandchildren will starve to death this winter. Now, go inside and find the girl!"

The old man paused, then said, "I went inside a moment ago to pray. There were only old women in there, I swear."

"I will kill you if you lie to me," the rough voice said.

Mina heard the tires crunch as he drove away. She panicked, not knowing what to do. *He will kill me next,* she thought. She was sure this voice came from the man with kohl-rimmed eyes named Haroon. Memories attacked her as she remembered what he had done to her, what he wanted to do again. She forgot everything in the tomb, even her prayers.

The darkened eyes of the man flooded back into her mind like a nightmare. She could not even blink. Her breath was quick and dry; she could not control it.

The sky was slowly turning dark as she sat in fear, huddled at the bottom of the wall. She wondered why the old man did not give her up to the terrible man. It was his life at risk now, too. A prayer returned to her, so she put her hand on the grave, prayed, and stood. The other women were crying and wiping their noses, preparing to leave for the night. Before they left the mausoleum one by one, they pulled on their burqas and covered their faces.

When the candles were no longer burning and the mausoleum was quiet, dark, and cold, Mina walked down the hill and sat on the last step. Soon, the old man with the muddy hands and shoes came and sat next to her. Mina looked at his face and wondered, *could this be Baba Wali? Is he not just a myth?* She wondered if this man was sent by God.

Maybe he worked during the day as a gardener and went back to his tomb at night? Her mind returned to quiet as she sat next to him;

they both observed the opium field under the orange reflection of the sunset.

The sticks of opium stood at attention in front of her like a thousand beaten men with kohl-rimmed eyes in a deep silence. They stared at her without blinking. She saw a trail of bloody opium mixing with the color of sunset as it crossed Elephant Mountain and illuminated the other side of the world.

The opium farm guard walked Mina to her house to make sure she was safe. He said, "My dear daughter, never come to this mausoleum again. You are in danger here. Someone bad knows where you pray." He looked at her with kind eyes and waved his wrinkled hands in the air. His dry, dusty lips moved slowly in silent prayer as he smiled, bowed, and headed back to the opium farm.

Chapter 2

Peacock

The man spoke to Mina, but she could not hear him; she was too distracted by his eyes, one that stared straight at her as the other darted continuously around the room. This made Mina nervous, but then again, everything made Mina nervous.

The man also spit in a continuous spray as he spoke. His voice was raspy, and the room echoed. Soon, he stopped talking. Mina thought perhaps he had become self-conscious.

Then he took a sip of his green tea and continued, "We cannot hire you here. No upstanding employer in this city can hire you. Women like you should stay home and listen to their elders. Kandahar is a small city, and you are meant to be home."

"But your organization is helping people who are victims of the war, isn't it? I want to be a part of that. I'm only here to help people." Mina looked at him as she spoke and then looked away again.

"Yes, we help victims of the war, but this is a man's job. For men only. You must understand this by now."

Mina stared at a stopped clock on the wall behind him. The clock needle was stuck at 4:27, but she did not know when it had stopped: years ago, months ago, hours ago? *Maybe it shows the time of the man's thoughts,* she said to herself. *Maybe this was when his words made sense.*

The man got up from his chair and limped toward her. He looked like a dry tree that had burned from the inside but still moved in the wind. His hands were shaking as he put his fingers under Mina's cheeks and looked straight into her face with his one able eye. "A pretty girl like you must stay home and marry someone soon." He paused. "A woman should be like a peacock. Have you ever seen peacocks fly far? Let go of ambitious flying. There is no space for this. There is not even space for a female hawk, only traps. Now, go, be a peacock." He turned away, gesturing wildly with his hands. "I have no idea what is going on in this office. I have already said there are no jobs here for women. Yet they still advertise this," he mumbled. "But I am not even the hiring manager; I am only here to interview you, and you are not a real candidate. If you have issues with this, you can ask for the boss tomorrow. Now, go home."

Mina was shocked by her father's face. The fatigue of war and endless gossip of the people in their small town had grooved deep, uneven lines into it. He was organizing dry sticks for the winter fire in the basement when a sharp piece of wood cut into his hand. He tried to pull it out with his teeth. Mina noticed how his whole body shook as she swept.

The smell of the cut sticks and green tea filled the basement. Light shone in from the small windows at the top of the walls and glinted off the fragments of wood and dust floating in the air. The winter in Kandahar was short, but her father was terrified of the cold in the house. He soothed his fear in the basement by collecting the sticks.

Once he was finished, he put on his white cotton hat and admired the walls lined with stacks of wood surrounding him. "We are ready," he said with a satisfied look. He sat on a stack of tanbarks and sipped his green tea without looking at Mina. "I saw that you went to get hired by that coward of a man. I know him well; he used to be the Taliban's commander with a beard down to his belly button. Now, he is the same person. He shaved his beard and wore a suit, but his attitude never changed." He sighed. "The stupid never change—they just change their color in the face of money and position. But I ask you now, why must you step on a beehive?"

She was quiet as she continued to push the broom into corners and under stacks where she could.

Her father's eyes were red. "I don't care what people say about me. I don't care if they think I'm a coward. I am not saying any of this for myself. I am saying this for you, Mina. I see how the men look at you. I know what they say. I know they want you to be someone you are not."

She looked at her father; he always spoke the truth. He wanted her to be safe, but he also knew she would not give up and become someone she was not.

The next afternoon, she went to the office again. She arrived at the same time as the boss and followed him in. The office smelled of dust and tobacco. The boss was a tall man with an ill-fitting brown suit. He took off his coat and hung it on the back of the chair. "My assistant said something about you yesterday I didn't quite get." Then he smiled and said, "Don't mind the old man; he's not used to working around women. I am the one who would choose to hire you or not." He coughed and sat in his chair. He leaned forward and steepled his hands. "I realize how desperate you are to get this job. You are quite brave." He clapped slowly a few times.

She closed her eyes and swallowed her disgust. The orange light of the room had mixed with his cigarette smoke and made the boss's face shine. Mina's résumé and application lay on the desk, but the boss did not look at them. His eyes were locked on her like a scanner.

"Will you hire me then? I can do all the computer work. I speak fluent English, Pashto, and Dari, and I can start tomorrow," she said.

The boss laughed, "Don't be impatient; you will work soon enough." He took another cigarette out of his pocket and lit it. His face got lost in the smoke. The ashes fell on her paperwork. He pushed them into the corner of his desk and said, "Your job here will be easy. Too easy! Nothing will be difficult if you just listen to me." He slowly walked toward her with his hands in his pockets. His foot kicked a crack in the cement floor several times as he stood close to her.

The silence was only broken by the noise of his shoes. Mina's eyes were frozen open. She felt scared and realized why; the boss reminded her of Haroon. She wanted to run away, but she hesitated; she wanted so badly to find a job—to prove to herself and the world that she could.

The spell was broken when he exhaled a thick cloud of smoke. She blinked and ran out of the office without picking up her papers. A taxi was waiting on the corner, and she jumped in it.

The taxi driver pulled forward and slowed next to a tree. He spit the green tobacco from under his tongue onto it. His head moved slowly, and his lips curled. He didn't seem well.

"You are alone?" he asked. He stared at her in the rearview mirror. Mina wanted him to look at the road. "Are you working there?" Again, she did not answer. "I can tell by your shoes you're a young woman." She pulled her burqa forward to hide them. "Now, let me see your face." She did not move. "I drive a lot of women. They are all working alone like you. I know your type well, you women who work outside the home." He smiled then and cocked his head with crazy eyes. He wiped his face on his scarf. "It's a warm evening? Do you want to go get some cold drinks?"

Mina couldn't take it anymore. "Stop this instant! Let me out of the car!" she yelled.

The driver lost control and hit the sidewalk. He threw the car into park and kicked open his door.

"My taxi isn't for whores like you! Go work outside to find rich men and keep your filth from my car!"

Mina's mouth was dry. She got out quickly, took off her shoes, and ran home as fast as she could. The rocks on the ground, the suffocating heat, the weight of her burqa as it pulled on her head and neck, she could barely feel any of it. She only knew the fear that kept her running.

When she arrived home, she stormed into her room and locked herself in. Her mouth was so bitter. She put her head on her pillow. Her long hair was stuck to her neck by sweat and tears. She squeezed her eyes closed. She felt like a convict being hung by a soft rope. Slowly, it closed around her neck until she found herself floating in a sticky darkness toward the terrible man with eyes rimmed in oval upon oval of black.

Chapter 3

Prison

"Mina can't do anything; she can't go anywhere. Not even Baba Wali is safe for her, even though there are plenty of other women around," Mina's mother said.

The smell of fried onions and lamb wafted into Mina's room, but she was not hungry. She was exhausted but couldn't sleep. She listened to her parents' conversation from her bed, her eyes closed.

"She can't get a job; she can only be jailed here, inside our home." Mina could hear the tears in her mother's voice.

After a long pause, her father said, "Someday soon, I will kill him. I swear it."

Mother continued, "Mina isn't like the other girls in Kandahar. She doesn't want to get married and have kids and stay home for the rest of her life. If she does this, she will gradually die; I can see this."

Mina heard the wooden spoon stirring, mixing, moving the lamb so it would cook evenly.

"But Mina does not want to die in this way." Her mother's voice got louder. "She wants to live! She wants to love and be loved, not live like a dead woman!"

Her father interrupted inside his own conversation. "I knew that bastard. He has stopped my daughter from living her life. I don't care if he's friends with the governor; I don't care about any of it. I will kill him, one way or another!"

Mina rolled over to look at the ceiling, a prisoner in her cell. As her parents became quiet, she could hear a song from the radio in the living room.

Let's leave this city, you, and me...
You take my hands, and I will take yours.
Let's go somewhere, otherwise we both will die.
Me because of not having you and you because of loneliness.

The song lingered in her mind after it ended. Suddenly, a different voice boomed from the radio.

"Kandahar prison is looking for female teachers for female inmates. If you are interested, call this number."

Mina's eyes popped open. She jumped from her bed. It was perfect! The answer she had been praying for. Her mother was a teacher, and she had helped in her classroom many times. The angels in the prison would bring her back to life, all while keeping her protected from Haroon. She needed these women as much, maybe more, than they needed her.

It was early morning; the air smelled of fresh bread. The road was filled with bicycles, cars, carriages, and buses jostling for position on the narrow main street. Students were hanging from the backs of buses as passengers smashed against each other inside. A teen boy stood on a seat and yelled, "Hand me your fare or I'll kick you onto the street!" Mina handed the boy her afghani and jumped from the bus as it slowed to a stop.

"Identification." The prison guard looked at her with puffy eyes and a skinny face. She opened her bag and gave her card to the guard. He yawned. "It's too early for your appointment. Wait here," he said, and showed her a dusty, broken chair in the corner of the guard cottage.

Finally, she found herself in the prison superintendent's office. It was the moment she had been waiting for, only it felt much like the moments leading up to it. The superintendent was silent as he pulled a pen from his uniform pocket while glaring at her. The nostrils of his large, wide nose were gun barrels targeting Mina with their fury. "You are going to be a teacher here, correct?" He did not wait for her to answer and looked at his assistant. "The foreigners are to blame for this foolishness." He shook his head, then looked at her over his glasses. "A pretty young girl like you should not be in this hell. It is the Americans who create this problem, and why? Why must they get everything they want? Female teachers are not wanted here—you should go!"

His assistant stood behind him in his crisp, dark green uniform. He leaned forward and whispered something in his ear.

The superintendent's nostrils flared, and his lips curled as he pulled Mina's paperwork toward him and signed in several places. "You will start tomorrow," he growled. "Nobody is willing to work in this dump except you; you are the first and last woman to apply for this stupid job. You will see tomorrow morning what a mistake you have made."

Dear Mina,

Congratulations on your new position in the Female Inmate's Literacy Training Project in Kandahar Prison supported by a non-government organization. My name is Rebecca. I am working in the Women's Empowerment Organization and heard about your important project in prison. As an American woman who works for the empowerment of women,I would like to register you in my organization and be your mentor. I am excited to welcome you into your new role. Attached, please find Part One of the training materials, including the curriculum I will be teaching and several assignments on how to balance your work and personal life and how to lead other women. Once you complete Part One of your training online, there will be a test in English. If you pass this test, you will become eligible to visit the U.S. for leadership training with the Women's Empowerment Organization. As your mentor, I would be hosting your stay here.

Please contact me if you have any questions or concerns about the material, your role, or if you just want to talk. I look forward to working with you and hopefully meeting you here in Washington, D.C.

Best regards,
Rebecca
Communications Coordinator

Mina tapped her fingers on her desk a few times while her hand under her chin portrayed her thoughts as she began her first day of work. She asked herself, *what if all these great programs for women had been arranged years before? Maybe Kandahar wouldn't have female prisoners if girls were educated. How is it possible that for many years, girls couldn't go to school, and now some of them, jailed in their own town, start learning the alphabet as adults in prison? Was that fair?* She felt a deep gap that made her heart empty and her thoughts disarranged. She pushed away all those thoughts and tried to focus on answering Rebecca's email properly.

Dear Rebecca,

Thank you very much for these materials. I am so proud and excited to participate in your educational programs for women as a student to learn more and support my students better; it is perfect for me. I will work hard and study to pass all the tests. I hope I can meet you soon.

Sincerely,
Mina

On the first day of her job as a teacher, the twelve girls in her class looked at her with frightened eyes. The guard stood by the door, and their eyes darted from him to Mina and back again. They looked like wounded deer trying to evade the hunter.

The guard stepped out and closed the door. Once he was gone, Mina took a deep breath and looked around her. The girls were so young to her, young and sad. Their heads hung low, looking at their feet. Mina gently cleared her throat. They sat quietly on the dusty ground staring only at her now. Mina looked at the moldy, crypt-like walls surrounding them and smiled, then sat cross-legged in front of them. "Today, let's write a letter to someone we love, girls." She said in her most spirited and upbeat voice that she could muster. "It can be your mother, your brother or sister—anyone." Mina paused then, in thought. *When had these young ladies last seen their mothers?* "You can tell them about your life here or tell them anything at all." Mina swallowed her sorrow.

The sad faces filled with big, beautiful smiles and Mina knew this was what it felt like to be lotus flowers blooming in a swamp.

Chapter 4

Pomegranate

A dark shadow followed her home from the prison. She could feel it. Mina looked over her shoulder repeatedly as she picked up her pace. She could never see it, but she knew it was there. She felt the toe of her right foot collide with a sharp rock, but she did not feel the associated pain. Warm blood flowed onto her sandal, and she began to run. When she turned to look for the shadow, she noticed the trail of blood droplets she had left on the street. Out of breath, she slowed and then stopped to untie the scarf from her neck and wind it around her toe. She kicked dirt over the line of blood and continued running.

Like heat pulsing from an oven, the sun blazed both outside and inside her head. What would she do if the shadow caught her? She was halfway home when she began knocking on the doors of strangers, praying for someone to open one. She knocked again and again. A dark gray lizard ran between cracks in the dirt like a maze. *Was she in a maze, too?* The lizard stopped to push off the hot ground, his white belly pounding up and down, up, and down. She stopped to knock on another door. It didn't matter how hard she knocked, no one would answer. It was as though the city were deserted—a ghost town with only Mina, the lizard, and the man who followed her.

Windows and doors were chained closed along the entire street; fear of war made the inhabitants do this. War drove them to do so many things they had never done before and would not have done otherwise. But still, she prayed a woman would answer the door. She knocked so many times that her knuckles started to chafe and redden. Sweat was running from her scalp and neck to her back. Even as her body was wet, she could feel the dust between her teeth.

Haroon was getting closer; she could hear his footsteps now. They felt like a gun barrel pressing hard against her temple. Death was waiting for her on every corner of the city like a trigger waiting to be pulled. But Mina did not fear death. Her only fear was of what people would do to her if she died on the street. Would they spit on her? Would they call her a whore? Mina worried more about her parents; could they bear the shame if she died in this way? Her feet were heavy; she felt like she was wading through thick mud instead of running on a dry street. How would she stay safe from the terrible man who had followed her all the way from the prison?

She turned down a quiet alley. Normally, there would be children playing, laughing joyfully, and street vendors calling out their wares. But this time of day, there was no noise. No one would choose to be outside during the last and hottest month of summer when the sun's heat acted like a laser through all things.

Out of the corner of her eye, she saw a pomegranate cart tucked in the shadow of an old white berry tree. Something moved under it; she thought it was probably an animal. As she moved closer, she could see it was an aged man, crippled and tired, resting from the heat. She pulled up her burqa to show him her face, sweaty from fear and desperate to escape the shadow. He smiled with kindness, showing her his few teeth. "Quick! Get under the cart!" he said. As she scrambled down to crawl under the cart, he draped wet cotton bags on the perimeter to cover her. Her nostrils filled with the smell of rotten pomegranate as she heard the man call out, "Pomegranate juice, fresh, cold, sweet! Only ten afghani!"

She worried that her breathing could be heard. Even though she tried, she couldn't make it go slower and softer. She pushed her scarf into her mouth as she heard the voice of the terrible man.

"No one is buying smelly pomegranate juice from a filthy old man like you! Now, tell me, have you seen a woman pass by?" She could never forget the voice. It felt like forever since she hadn't heard it in her nightmares. Thousands of times she heard him, remembering his unpleasant breath, feeling the burning pain from inside brought on by memories of him.

She was so lost in her thoughts and the echo of his words in her head that she didn't hear him lose control and punch the cart in anger.

"No one is outside on a hot day like today," the pomegranate peddler said to him. "No one has come by me, woman or man. Now go along and let me do my business."

The man kicked the cart several times. It shook but did not collapse, even though it was old and rickety. Sour red juice dripped through the cracks in the wood and mixed with the sweat on her skin. She was hot yet shivered. Her skin flinched when the cold drops of juice landed on her.

Her mind went blank, and she suddenly felt herself dreaming while wide awake. She felt the piercing pain of her bones breaking apart and her skin being torn to shreds. She could sense warm blood oozing from her body even though it wasn't time for her monthly cycle. She continued chewing her scarf as her whole body shook from inside. She didn't know how much time had passed when she heard the peddler man say, "He is gone now; you can come out, girl."

She peered out like a frightened animal. Her hair and neck were sticky and red with pomegranate juice. Her eyes burned from the red drops that had landed in them. As she came to stand in front of the old man, she knew he—his actions and words—would be stamped in her mind forever. "Pomegranate juice, fresh, cold, sweet! Only ten afghani!"

The peddler's voice swirled in her head as she walked into her home. The sun had set, and the first star of the night could be seen above Kandahar like a silver beacon.

Her father was watering the grape trees as he did every night. She could hear the water rising in the pipes and pouring onto the ground, disappearing into the thirsty soil. She knelt and dropped her head under the cold, fresh water from the hose. She wanted to stay there, to be baptized from her memories and cleansed for hours, all her stress and worries rinsed away. She felt her father's hand on her shoulder. "He followed you again today," he said. She looked at him in shock as he continued. "You know what? No one should see you or know what you are doing. I told you many times, you should not be out in this city, working, walking, but you will not learn this. I will find you dead one day because you won't stay home." He slammed the shovel into the soil. "Whatever I say is nothing to you. You shouldn't want this to end with your bloodshed."

She wiped the water from her face with her sleeve as he kicked the dry leaves and ranted on.

"Do you understand we live in Kandahar? How many wars must we see before we stop creating more worries for ourselves? We have no more tears to cry for you. You must stop your dangerous choices."

Mina finally spoke. "Didn't you teach me to go after what is precious? I don't want to hide! I want to work! To help!" He would not look at her as she spoke, but she knew he understood who she was and who she would always be.

Chapter 5

Erick

Mina opened the classroom door slowly while her mother was writing the homework for her students on the black board at the end of class. She wiped the chalk dust from her hands on a rag as the bell rang. The second-grade girls screamed happily and ran out.

As she sat behind her mom's desk, waiting for her to finish, a row of new coloring pencils got her attention. She hadn't seen new pencils in a long time.

"Where did you get these?" she asked as she picked one up.

"An American soldier brought them here; his name is on the pencils in English."

Mina turned the pencil. "Erick? Who is Erick?"

"I have no idea, but he sent a lot of pencils to this school. I am grateful to him."

"Why did he carve his name on these pencils? The Taliban will find out who he is, and he will be in great danger," Mina said.

"Or maybe it's a trap, and the pencils will be how he catches them," her mother said. They both laughed. "He must be smart and kind. The other soldiers bring snacks for the girls. Pencils are much more useful. He is looking out for us." She opened the drawer of her desk like she was hiding treasure. "Pick a pencil for yourself and one for each of your students. I have a lot now." Mina watched a line of pencils roll back and forth with Erick's name appearing and disappearing as they rolled.

A dark green prison guard truck stopped by the inspection post at the Kandahar airport entrance. The young local Afghan police jumped from the back seat of the truck and opened the car door for Mina and the prison superintendent. Inspection police saluted the superintendent, standing at attention. Mina saw the wonder on his face behind the burqa, a local officer with a dusty hat. He told the superintendent loudly, "The commander is waiting for you."

The American commander was the biggest man she'd ever seen; she did not know how he could fit his body into the uniform that displayed the American flag proudly on his massive chest. His office was at the Kandahar airport on the opposite side from where the domestic flights would land. Mina and the prison superintendent were called to visit him that day.

"Mina, with your efforts all year, our female inmates have learned to read and write. We are very pleased with your work, and you have done quite well on your tests so far," the commander said.

"Yes, we have done many things to help our female prisoners," the superintendent chimed in.

The commander looked at him and smiled, then looked at Mina. "We are so appreciative of your hard work in this prison and the dedication to your studies. We would like to extend the literacy project for another year. You have made this program a success." He handed the paperwork to the superintendent, who squinted at her and signed them.

Mina was looking for a pen in her bag and noticed the pencils with Erick's name carved on them. They had signed the contract, and the meeting was almost finished, but Mina was curious: who was this, Erick?

As they were leaving, she asked the commander, "Is there a man here named Erick?"

The commander smiled. "I know Lieutenant Erick. He's an army guy; I think he's a peacekeeper. Why? Do you know him?"

"No, no, I do not know him at all."

The commander smiled again. "We have your work email address. I can send you his if you'd like."

It was midnight as Erick sat behind the broken, muddy wall. Only the sounds of crickets could be heard in the Arghandab village he was guarding. Crickets and the occasional gurgle of water flowing into the rows of the vineyard next to him. The wind brought the fresh smell of eucalyptus trees. This fragrance was familiar to him from before his time in Kandahar; he knew when the leaves burned, it smelled like perfume had been sprayed in the air. Now the smell of eucalyptus trees would always remind him of this town.

His body was in terrible pain; he had been stuck in the same position for hours. His knees were asleep, and he could feel nothing below them. The dust was heavy on his eyelashes and was giving him a headache. Sometimes, insects from the vineyard would jump onto his face. *Maybe they think I'm dead*, Erick thought. He could feel the insect's legs running on his nose, but he could not move. Both his hands were on his gun. His skin burned from sweat as much as it had when he got his first tattoo. But that was a long time ago, and he hadn't cared about the stinging at the time.

The eucalyptus scent wafted in again and reminded him of the day his friend died. They were in the Registan Desert south of Kandahar; gusty winds and extreme heat had come from nowhere, and winds blew over the moon-shaped dunes. He remembered his friend looking at the anemometer. "Hey, Erick, look! This crazy wind always blows from west to south; the direction never changes. Interesting, huh?"

He could still hear the roaring sands of the Registan Desert in his ears. It sounded like a stringed instrument playing a single note over and over, a note that could be heard from far away.

It seemed that day evil spirits had played with a billion grains of sand, colliding them together, causing them to roar. For a little while, nobody could see anything. Then Erick opened his burning eyes and saw his friend's body blown apart all over again. He had collected all the pieces of him in a black plastic bag, which he zipped and pushed into the stomach of the military airplane heading for home, heading for a coffin covered in red, white, and blue.

Erick's eyes filled with tears. He knew he would leave this bloody city soon, but first he needed to stay awake all night to ensure that the Taliban would not bury another bomb under the skin of the road, blowing apart another American—or civilian. In that dark night, he was drowned in his thoughts as he noticed some movement in the shadows.

What the fuck are they doing? He thought to himself. The sky was lightening as morning got closer. He felt the trigger with his finger. He was ready to kill those moving shadows, but his thoughts were interrupted when his captain spoke to him from his headphones.

"If you see anyone suspicious, do not kill them; we need them alive. I repeat, do not kill anyone." Erick breathed deeply and rested his gun on the broken wall.

It was a summer night, one of those nights that came maybe once a year. The weather was fresh, and Mina's window was open. The wind brought the scent of sea-buckthorn into her room. The trees were the only thing she liked about her home. She wasn't sure why, but they gave her happiness. Moonlight shone in a line on her floor and onto her computer desk. She turned on her laptop, and only one thing came into her mind.

Dear Erick,

You may be wondering who I *am*? You have never met me. I only know you because of your kindness. Our students and the teachers who received your pencils are so grateful. For us, a pencil is a symbol of wisdom, truth, and freedom. With this gift, you encouraged our girls to continue their education even at the hardest time. The pencils with your name carved into them have motivated our girls, and even me, to move forward for education, freedom, and our rights as women. I am a teacher in the Female Inmate's Literacy Training Project; do you know about this program? My students and I will use your pencils every day to further ourselves and our education.

Thank you again,

Mina

She sent the email without a clue where Erick would be when he received it, but the pencils were stuck in her mind like a mysterious secret she wanted to unravel. She lay in bed and closed her eyes. She even forgot to turn off her computer. She felt so good for no reason—so relaxed. She yearned to save this unique feeling in her mind forever. She did not expect a quick response, but her computer pinged.

Hello Mina,

Your email made my day, and I'm so glad to see it. I believe in the girls of Kandahar, and I'm happy you are one of the people who received the pencils. I know the girls in Kandahar weren't allowed to go to school for years because of their gender, but now I hope it's getting better. I'm so glad I got to see the girls taste freedom. I wish all the people in the world knew how much passion girls in Kandahar have for learning. I have heard of your project, and I believe you are one of those girls who can lead other women to their freedom and rights in the future. How is Kandahar? I have missed it since I left.

Respect,

Erick

Chapter 6

Talib

The neighbors and their children were screaming; the kitchen windows rattled. Mina turned off the oven, put the cover over a brown rice dish, and ran to the yard.

At first, she thought neighbors would catch an animal and bring it into their home to prepare it for cooking. But when she got closer, she saw a man with dirty clothes and a bloody face sitting in the middle of the yard, his hands tied with a rope. Children surrounded him and some of them hit him with sticks.

Father yelled at all of them and said, "Go away! Leave him alone. Let me see who he is."

Our neighbor came over and proudly said, "He is a Talib boy. We just caught him before he exploded himself in the crowded Bazar, since it is too late, and nobody is in the police station now, we brought him here until morning." The neighbor man covered his fingers across his scalp. "He must be hanged. He almost killed hundreds of people." He dropped his hands down and looked away from the dirty man.

Then the neighbor hit his back sharply with the wooden stick. Father pushed him away and said, "What are you doing? Are you blind? He is captive now." Turning to the other neighbors he asked them to take the Talib boy to the basement.

Men pulled him on the ground, and together they drug him to the basement. In a moment the yard became empty like the yard had swallowed all of the men and Talib boy together. After a few minutes the neighbors came out of the basement one by one. They looked calm, put their hands on their chest, talked slowly with Father, then left the house one by one.

Mina stealthily witnessed, through the basement window, the Talib boy and her father talking. Mina couldn't hear anything, just felt everything was calm now and the atmosphere was better.

Father came out from the basement and told Mina, "Go prepare a big plate of food for the Talib boy. He must be very hungry," he smiled. Grinning, he added, "Mina, not a plate your stomach size. Make it for a hungry Talib boy's stomach."

Father pulled up his white shirt sleeves and washed his face with hose water for sunset prayer. Mina rushed to the kitchen and picked up a big pot filled with brown rice, lamb, raisins, and nuts with carrot slices. Then she filled a large, copper glass with cold water and put it all together in a big platter with a big piece of warm naan.

Father came to the kitchen after praying and said, "I will give him the food." Then noticed Mina and said, "You want to give the Talib his food? It is okay if you can take the food to the basement. He is too weak to hurt you and his hands are fastened tightly." Father put his hand in his pocket and pulled out a small yellow key. Handing it to Mina he said, "Here, it's to the basement. Go take his food," Father slid the plate upon a tray. "I will untie his hands after praying. But be careful."

Mina's feet were shaking, as were the dishes in her hands, as she went to the basement, but she was curious to see a Talib closely.

The short door of the basement rumbled. She turned on the light and saw a boy scared and pulling back, trying to blend into the wall. Mina's hands shook and dishes rattled. She put the food slowly on the floor and said, "My father sent you this food. He will untie your hands in a few minutes, okay? It's Qabeli Pallaw."

She saw the Talib boy with dark green, wild eyes sparkling in the basement light. His long, black hair surrounded his shoulder, and his lips were bloody. It seemed someone hit his mouth. Dry blood was on his forehead and his long, black beard. His skinny body, in large, black clothes, was like a scarecrow in the middle of an abandoned farm. When she saw his face, she was not scared anymore. He wasn't even as scary as Haroon was.

Mina asked him, "How old are you?"

Talib said, "I don't know, maybe seventeen."

Warm food smells filled the basement; Mina wanted to leave.

The Talib boy's voice quietly cracked as he asked, "Water. Water. Give me some water..." Mina looked at his hands and feet tightly bound with a rope. She picked up the copper glass of water and lifted it close to the Talib boy's dry, bloody, and dusty lips. He drank the whole glass with closed eyes, sipping from Mina's shivering hands.

Mina held the empty glass at her side and said angrily, "Why were you going to kill yourself and other people today in the bazaar? Why did you become a Talib? Why did you join the Taliban?"

Talib was quiet for a while then said, "God ordered me. I must obey God." Then rubbed his wet, bloody lips to his shoulder, glancing at Mina. "Mulla, my leader! Mulla ordered me to kill the Americans; their vehicle parked close to the bazaar today. That's why I wanted to blow them up—because Americans are infidel and transgressive."

Not satisfied with his answer, and not scared anymore of the tiny Talib boy who thought you must be killing because of

God,Mina asked, "Why doesn't Mulla blow himself up for God and kill Americans—and why does he ask you to do that?"

She continued, "How does Mulla know Americans are infidel? They also believe in God, but they have a different religion. If they don't believe in God, they are not going to sleep in the same grave with Mulla after death. Does God punish them by putting them together in the same grave? Why did you trust Mulla's words? Think! Listen to what your mind tells you. Why are they transgressive? That is not why they came in our country." Mina kept her eyes upon the Talib boy, "They came here to help to keep the peace."

The boy's eyes didn't move, he just listened to Mina. With his lips shivering and tears in his eyes, he said, "I don't know. I don't know why Americans are here. I do not know why I must kill them. I do not know why I am here."

They both cried.

Mina asks, "Do you have any family? Mom, Dad, brother, sister?"

The Talib boy shook his head, "No, nobody. Mulla found me from the mosque when I was a newborn baby and raised me for God to become in God's service. It's not only me—Mulla raised thousands of kids like me, and all are in God's service now."

Mina asked, "Mulla raised you and other kids to become killers? Why do you trust Mulla? Are you sure he came from God? Are you sure he is God's man?"

Talib seemed shocked, as if by the high voltage power stick on the wall and didn't even blink. He looked like he didn't hear Mina anymore, or he was in a different world. Or couldn't understand her.

She picked up the little key from her dress pocket saying, "My dad will come soon to release your hands."

The Talib boy said, "Wait, wait... listen, I don't have a strong father like yours, or mom, house, warm food, roof over my head, siblings, or a sister like you to give me a glass of water. I do not have anything. Understand? If I do not have anything, then why must I be alive? Life doesn't have any meaning to me because I don't have anything. Maybe after dying, as Mulla said, in the other world, I would have mom, dad, family, warm food, and a roof at the top of my head. Maybe after death I don't have to stay in the cold winter and hot summer as a guard dog outside of Mulla's house while starving to death. Maybe I don't have to carry a heavy bag of weapons and explosive things on my back from village to village, mountain to mountain, for Mulla—for a piece of bread. Maybe dying is thousands of times sweeter than the life I have right now. Maybe Mulla's promises are true, and I would have a better life in the other world. I wanted the suicide vest to explode myself to go to the other world faster. Now, you tell me, if you were me, wouldn't you choose the suicide vest over this kind of life?"

Mina couldn't take it anymore. She ran to the door. Then, father saw her sad face and asked, "What happened? Did he hurt you?"

"No, nothing happened. Please open his hands before his food becomes cold. But promise me, do not let the neighbors hit him tomorrow morning when you take him to the police."

Father, surprised, said, "You do not have to be worried; you know me very well. I won't punish anybody before his crime is confirmed. That is why neighbors brought him to me. I won't let any injustice happen. Trust me."

That night Mina's appetite was gone. She prepared dinner, but she couldn't eat as she remembered the Talib boy's desperate face. She felt sick knowing how the young man became a toy boy of Mulla's. How can a human being abuse another in the name of God? Talib had put his faith in God under question and she couldn't even believe God could be this cruel.

Chapter 7

Registan

*T*he prison guard in his green uniform opened her classroom door roughly. The girls in their purple uniforms and white scarves jumped back.

"You!" The guard pointed at Mina. "Come here. The boss wants to speak to you."

Mina was not expecting a meeting, especially not in the middle of her class time, but she obeyed and followed the guard.

In his office, the prison superintendent twisted his hands behind his neck and leaned back in his chair. His legs were propped on his desk, and he looked at the ceiling. "Sit down," he said without looking at Mina. "We are waiting for one other person."

"Who?" she asked nervously. "What is this about?"

The superintendent did not answer. The ceiling fan turned slowly as a big black beast of a fly sat on the fan's center.

"I never should have hired a woman," he muttered as he looked at his watch. Right then, a man in a brown vest and shoes and white shirt walked into the office. The superintendent jumped from his chair. They hugged each other and then exchanged a pointed eye.

The new guy sat beside Mina, opened his notebook, and crossed his legs. He began to speak. She noticed his accent was not from Kandahar. He was from Afghanistan, but somewhere beyond her city's borders.

"There are some complaints about you at this prison. I have come from the religious council to take care of this issue before they send your complaint letter to the court. You knew your work was against the rules of our religion, correct?"

Mina's tongue locked. She looked at his face; his eyes were also rimmed in kohl, which made her want to flee, but this time it was different. It felt like the office was suspended in space, and she was staggering, moving in a gap beyond it. This made her dizzy.

"Do you know why these girls are here at this prison? Because they disobeyed. Women must always obey their husbands, fathers, brothers, and uncles, but these women did not. They escaped from their families because they fell in love." The man smiled. "Such a good excuse! Love!" He shook his head and spat at the ground. "These stupid women had secret relations with men outside of their homes without permission. Some of them were widows who got pregnant! And now they want you to find their children!"

"No," Mina said. "I am not searching for their children. One of my students is currently pregnant; she talked about her pregnancy with me yesterday. That is all."

The man yelled, "Who cares if she is pregnant?" His face turned red. "Are you their teacher or their doctor? Stop talking to these stupid girls! They are all guilty. They will stay in this prison until their hair turns white and their teeth fall out. They are followers of Satan, and like Satan, they disobeyed God. Did you know Satan first tricked Eve? Then Adam disobeyed God because of Eve? Do you know most hellions are women?"

Mina was silent for a moment, then finally asked, "How do you know most hellions are women? Have you counted all the hellions?" She forced herself to be calm, to not raise her voice for fear of what might happen. "You are spying on me; this makes you also guilty. I am only a teacher at this prison. Sometimes after class the girls talk to me as a student talks to their teacher, nothing more. I only listen to them—that is all."

The man's face turned red like fire. He looked at the prison superintendent. "See? She is foolish! She has offended a religious man—a man of God. Why didn't you tell me she is also disrespectful?"

"She is so young," the superintendent said. "She hasn't learned to honor religious men." He looked at Mina then; disgust filled his eyes. "A religious man is not a sinner. This man is pure. Only he has the power to understand right from wrong, good from bad."

The man stood and walked in front of her chair. "You teach these girls to disobey men. And furthermore, you are spying for them. This is against our laws. You are guilty of sins and must be punished. If you still want to work here, do not speak to these women other than teaching or you will be summoned to Sharia court to become a prisoner yourself! Or sent back to the Registan Desert to suffer and die!" He threw the door open and stormed out.

Mina was dizzy. She did not want to listen to anything more the superintendent had to say. She stared at the fan until her eyes lost focus and the fly was a black smear. She thought he was pretending to be dead.

When she stepped out of the prison that day, it felt like she entered a different world. The people and the city were unknown to her. She was born there, in the same house as her mother and grandmother, but she felt like a stranger—victimized by the city that used to be Kandahar. This Kandahar, with its three thousand years of history and civilization, was unrecognizable. Shame on all ancient cities with beautiful, meaningful histories if this is what they come to, if this is how they treated women in the end. How had women suffered in this city thousands of years before her time here? What else must happen to come full circle on the history of Kandahar? She did not want to be an oppressed woman, read about in textbooks by future generations. She wanted to invalidate every rule ever created to cause women to be so poorly treated. She wanted to rise in freedom, her ears singing with the wind blowing through the sands of the Registan desert, the roar of change to bring freedom at last.

She walked on the streets like she was walking in an unknown land. Her feet pushed her to walk, but she had no more energy. Nothing mattered. She was no longer scared that Haroon would put his gun to her temple and pull the trigger. Her heart was empty.

When she arrived home, she did not want to see or talk to anybody. Like a thief, she tiptoed into the hallway.

"Why does your face look like a dead person?" her mother asked from behind her.

Mina did not turn around. "I think I have a fever; I don't feel good."

Her back shivered and her hands were shaking as she went into the bathroom and took off her clothes in front of the mirror. The smell of the prison, dark and moldy, filled her lungs. She could not breathe well; it felt like her lungs were filled with stones. She bit her lip and turned on the shower, then slipped and fell into the mirror with the full weight of her body. Pieces of glass cut her hands where she tried to stop herself, and blood seeped from her elbow. In the reflection of the glass shards on the floor, she saw thousands of men with kohl-rimmed eyes staring back at her nakedness.

In the shower, she removed a broken piece of glass from her foot. She felt no external pain. It was the pain no one could see or know about that consumed her.

At night, when she lay on her bed, her pregnant student Anargol, with her pale face and dry lips, came to her mind again. Each time Anargol feels nauseous in class, she presses her shawl to her mouth and closes her eyes. It was as if she wanted to bring up all the sorrows inside her. *No, it was not the baby in her womb that was bothering her*, she thought. *These damn days in prison made her sick.* But she'd always keep writing as she put her notebook on her knee.

Mina wanted to write a letter to the man who Anargol had run away from home because of and been jailed because of, but Anargol did not care about what happened to her. She keeps writing; it seems writing was the only way to connect her to her lover. And the alphabet—her rope to get her out of this prison.

Mina put her hands on her neck, breasts, stomach, and belly button. She felt as though her own womb was growing bigger, filled with her own pregnancy of pain. She envisioned the dark creatures in prison raping her, just like they did Anargol.

The winter rain hit the wooden windows, and some drops came into her room. She covered her head with a blanket, knowing even this heavy rain could not rinse her wounds. She wanted to scream—a yell that twisted with wind and dark clouds, made the rain heavier, and turned it into a killer storm. She wanted the rain to continue without stopping until it broke the prison walls and its locks, chains, and doors. She wished for the rain to clean all of Kandahar's wounds and rinse the whole world until the earth opened and swallowed all the nasty things in the city. Only a pure world would remain, pristine as it was on the first day God created it.

Chapter 8

Sanam

anam was sitting cross-legged in front of the beautician lady. The woman with a magnifying glass and skinny face put the cotton string on her mouth, made the string wet, rubbed it between her palms and targeted the hair between Sanam's eyebrows. With each hair strand she plucked, Saman's eyes watered. Then, the lady replaced her glasses and moved Sanam's face to the left and right side carefully. "Looks good!"

Then, she picked up a small silver tweezer from her corset and plucked hair from Sanam's upper lips. She showed the tweezer to Mina and said, "I can make you prettier than the bride. Just wait for a few minutes. I am almost done."

Mina was leaning on a green roll pillow beside the bride. "Thank you! I can do it by myself."

The beautician rolled her eyes and said, "As you wish!"

Sanam growled under her lips saying, "You are lucky to not have this much hair on your face, otherwise you would cry too on your wedding night." They both laughed and the lady said, "Stop shaking. I almost picked up the wrong hair from your eyebrow."

When the beautician left, Mina said quietly, "Is he handsome? Is he tall? What is his job? What is his style?"

"I don't know. I have never seen him at all. My parents just told me that he is a good guy. He also has never seen me."

Mina pushed her arm and said, "Are you crazy? Are you sure you want to marry someone you have never seen?"

Sanam, with worried eyes, looked around the room that was filled with women busy with their makeup and stated, "Whatever my parents say, I must listen. There is no option."

A woman with a huge red dress came close to Sanam, opened her handbag, and put a golden, heavy necklace on her neck and twelve bracelets on Sonam's hands. Then she put a golden star-shaped jewelry on the bride's nose and smiled ugly. She said, "Look, my daughter-in-law looks like a moon of the fourteenth night," then covered the bride's face with a green golden shawl.

Then another woman with burning harmala seeds came into the bride's room. A very nice smell filled the room, and it was even stronger than the women's perfumes and makeup smells.

She moved the burning harmala vase around Saman's head and other women sang songs together. "Go away ... groom is coming. The groom is coming...."

The women left the bride alone. Mina was the only brides-maid, and she moved just enough to make room beside the bride for the groom. Among the harmala smoke that filled the room a huge body came and sat beside Sanam. Mina thought he was the groom's father, but as soon as he sat down, he moved his hands under the bride's shawl and took Sanam's small hand in his big hands. Mina was shocked by seeing that act. How quick can a man touch a woman he has never seen before? Mina looked at the groom's face. He put his other hand on his wide stomach and black beard, and his tiny eyes smiled. The groom reminded Mina of Haroon somehow, and the panic attacked her. Bad feelings and trauma stirred within her again.

Rather than the groom, Mina wished she could leave that wedding room and escape with Sanam. Then, they both could go to Mina's house, bring the candies and snacks under her bed, eat, and laugh at the groom as much as they could. The wedding room's air, heavy and suppressing, encouraged her departure. Mina left the room and ran away. She knew Sanam would come to hate this guy. She was sure he wasn't the one Sanam wanted to marry, and on top of everything, he was even older than Sanam's father.

Mina ran to the kitchen and found her mom cooking rice and chicken in huge pots.

Mom asked, "What are you doing here? Go! Your clothes will smell of smoke and food. Go to the wedding room."

Mina replied, "But, Mom! You did not see the groom? He is too old for Sanam."

Mom removed her hands from her cooking and took Mina from the kitchen saying, "Stop yelling... I know. I know. But it's not our business. I told Sanam's mom several times that the groom is very old for her daughter, but she didn't listen to me. Sanam is their daughter, and they can do whatever they want for her. We cannot do anything. Understand? Do not ruin the wedding now. Go, be with your friend. At least she won't feel lonely tonight."

Mina went back to the wedding room. Sanam's shoulders were shivering under the shawl. Mina was sure Sanam feared this man that she had never seen before. And the worst part was that Sanam must sleep with him! The groom, his mother, the beautician lady, and all the other women in the wedding room looked like monsters that swallowed Sanam slowly. Mina left the room. She was looking for her shoes among all the women's shoes outside the wedding room, but she had lost them. She couldn't find her shoes, only red plastic slippers that she found in the corner. She threw them on and ran to the main door to leave the house.

She saw Sanam's dad behind the door. "Where are you going, girl? We're almost to serve dinner. Go back and stay with your friend. Sanam would be happy to have your company tonight."

There was no going back and forth. Mina was stuck at the wedding, and this was a thousand times worse than the prison cells she worked in every day.

Mina did not go back to the wedding room—she just stood on the balcony in front of the room. That groom's mother pulled away the curtains and said, "What are you doing here? Come, sit closer to the bride. You are a pretty girl, just like Sanam. The women in this room will pick you up tonight for their sons. Look at your friend; she found such a handsome groom tonight." Then she laughed loudly—her two front teeth covered with golden crowns shining in the lights.

Mina took off the plastic slippers and covered her face saying, "Thank you. The wedding room was so full of harmala smoke. Let me stay here to get fresh air."

That night, Mina felt she had fallen in a trap like a sparrow. But Sanam was stuck forever in the trap that her parents had made for her.

Chapter 9

Kabul

Mina still couldn't sleep. Her eyes were closed, but her nerves were unraveled. Unwanted thoughts continually smashed into her mind, all of them leading to Haroon, Sanam, and her students in prison. She could not trick herself into feeling calm. She sat up and threw her pillow, fighting her bedsheets. She rounded her scarf around her neck and stepped outside, slowly climbing the stairs to the roof. There was a single yellow light at the end of the street convulsing in the wind and rain. The sky lit with lightning, and she crunched herself down inside her shawl. Droplets of heavy rain bit her shoulders as she looked into the wind, her hair wild.

She was soaked when she walked down the stairs, entered the hall, and opened her mother's bedroom door. Her mom looked up while turning the pages of her students' papers. She cocked her head in concern.

"Come here," her mother said. Mina sat next to her. Her mother continued reading the papers as she said, "The rain will not help you now. When your mind is out of control, nothing can be solved." She took off her glasses. "I know wherever you go in the city, he is behind you like a shadow. And you are not a girl who can stay home and hide. I do not know exactly what to do with you." She sighed. "Go to sleep now, Mina, until sunrise. Tomorrow will be another day."

"What would you do if you were me?" Mina asked.

Her mom put her glasses back on and looked at her through them. "You cannot compare my life to yours. They are not equal in any way. We both live in Kandahar, in the same city, the same home, but nothing is the same. Everything has changed."

Mina wished she could explain her terror, her lack of sleep, how she felt him behind her even when he wasn't there, but she didn't want to worry her mom more, so she sighed and stayed silent. Her mom closed her eyes for a moment before she spoke again.

Mother leaned on the pillow, sipped her tea, and said, "Come closer my darling. Sometimes you act like an innocent girl. Well, you were born and raised in war. You didn't see the beauties of your hometown, but I did."

Mina put her head on her mother's knee and for a while Mother patted her long hair before she continued, "When the spring arrived in Kandahar before the wars, the Citrus aurantium trees around the house blossomed. The fragrance rose and spread everywhere, filling my lungs. At four o'clock, the flowers in the pond raised their heads as though they wanted to see their own reflections. You were born on the first night of the summer. I felt like there was no oxygen in my room, so I opened all the wooden windows and breathed deeply, inhaling the fragrance that lingered. Back then we didn't have the technology to see the gender, but I knew you were a baby girl. When you moved from side to side as I was enjoying the Citrus aurantium blossoms or listening to the birds and the sounds of the water in the pond, I knew you were dancing."

Her mother smiled. "I craved green, sour aloe; lemon; and green, fresh baby almonds with salt; all signs you were a girl. I walked slowly to the room at the end of the hall, the one with the balcony. We called it the 'Last Room.' I was born there. Your grandma was born there. And then, it was your turn to see all the beauty of this world and make all the wonderful memories, like we had, in the same house. Pain grabbed my back and stomach like a tiger's paws on a deer's neck. Only your grandma was with me as I cried that night. Your dad was working in Kabul. I looked up at the wooden beams on the ceiling. That wood still smells like newborn babies. Yes, wood has memories it stores; it saves the smell for a long time. I smiled as I heard the screams of my new baby girl."

Mother braided her long, gray hair as she spoke, rubbing in a small drop of essential oils just like she used to. The smell filled the room and made Mina think of her childhood. "Such beautiful days those were—nothing like today. Just a few months after you were born, Kandahar changed. We could hear the soldiers' boots outside and their yelling at night. The birds did not even sing, or if they did, we could no longer hear them. The weather changed, too—we had a drought for years; all trees died. This house was the only thing we had, and its basement was our shelter where we hid from the bombs."

Mother stopped patting Mina's hair then as she spoke, "Kandahar people don't laugh anymore. Our people used to be famous for smiling in conversation. I remember when I was your age, on my way home from school, I would pass the old, roofed bazaar every day. I remember the brown wooden baskets of wool, cotton, and silk. Dried fruits filled each corner of the bazaar, and the smell of henna, musk, and amber mixed with turmeric, cinnamon, cloves, and jujube, along with other colorful spices and perfumes. The salesmen had happy faces as they cleaned and organized their spice jars, and the men in the jewelry shops filled women's wrists with bangles—women who were not scared, who did not cover their faces as they bargained with salesmen. I felt like a butterfly with my light, white scarf floating around my neck as I ran through the bazaar and filled my arms with glass-colored bangles from wrist to elbow and laughed with girls as we raced to see how many we could fit on each arm."

She smiled as she continued, "Even the boys enjoyed shopping with us; they stopped to watch the girls' bangle races. At the time, boys and girls were in class together, in the same school, even sitting on the same bench. We were free to go to school and do many other things in Kandahar as women and as girls. Your grandfather loved his daughters more than his sons. On Friday nights, he would take me hunting. We hunted deer in the Registan. Sometimes, the roaring sands would fill my ears as we hunted. The deer would disappear in a blink, never to be seen again. Everyone would say no one comes back alive from a Registan sandstorm, but my father and I, we did. Kandahar felt like a corner of paradise when we went hunting! Your grandfather was an excellent hunter and an artist, too. When we came home, he brought his old box up from the basement and taught me calligraphy; we practiced together for many years." Mother rubbed her eyes. "Go to sleep, Mina. Now I will be awake with the memories until morning for both of us."

Mina left the room. The yard outside was dark; the sound of the raindrops hitting the walls of the yard could be heard. Winds had shut the doors. The neighborhood dogs barked loudly. She went to the room with the balcony, the one Mom called the Last Room where they now stored old boxes, shoes, and dresses. She turned the light on and felt all the babies in her family, boys and girls, all born in this room. She felt them looking at her, some of them dead like her grandma, some of them, her cousins and aunts, still alive at various ages living in different cities. Some of her grandma's babies were dead at birth, but Mina was still alive—there in the Last Room, the room where she was born. Mother always said the room smelled different, and Mina had never asked why. Now, she knew. She heard unfamiliar noises and shivered with goosebumps. She turned off the light and rushed to the kitchen. She poured hot water in a glass of ox tongue tea and mixed it with honey. She brought it back to her mom. "Drink this. It will help you sleep better tonight," she said. Her mom squeezed her hand and thanked her with her eyes.

Mina returned to her room, turned on her laptop, and waited for her computer to load. She was surprised by the email she saw and wondered if it was sent to the wrong person.

Dear Mina,

Congratulations on finishing Part One of the Leadership Program. You passed the online test. How is your literacy training in Kandahar prison? We thank you for the precious time you have spent on the education of women in your hometown. We are pleased with your success in the in-country management training; as you know, working hard while studying at the same time is no easy feat! It has been my pleasure to get to know you and follow your progress these last three months. Through our conversations, I have witnessed the tremendous effort you put toward your learning and education, and I am now thrilled to offer you an invitation to join our Leadership Training Program in Washington, D.C. You will stay at my home with me during this program; there is no need to concern yourself with room and board. I will contact you through email in the next few days to confirm your attendance and organize your trip.

Best regards,
Rebecca

Mina's eyes locked on the computer screen. Was it possible they invited a forgotten woman to America from the corner of Kandahar? She left her desk, went to the kitchen, turned on the stove, and filled the kettle with tap water while she was thinking about going to America...for what? Does her trip and training help other Afghan women? Why has America suddenly remembered forgotten Afghan women? Why didn't they hear us during the Taliban regime? Why have they abandoned us before and let our women become the hostages of extremists for so many years? Where were they when blood was dripping from Kandahar pomegranates? Why have they let us be tortured by the Taliban? For years, they chose to be silent. What if this is a temporary attention to Afghan Women? *Will* they forget about us in the future again? *Will* Americans stay in Afghanistan forever? What would happen if they left the country and the Taliban and extremist ideologies took over Afghanistan again? Should I trust them? She was drowning in her thoughts and touched the kettle handle with bare hands. Her fingers stung. She put her hand under the tap water until the stinging cooled down. After making her own tea, she went to talk to her mom again.

"I've been invited to America for training! I can go and stay with Rebecca, the lady who is working with me online in leadership training. I will see how women live there and learn something new!"

Mom put her finger to her lips where she was resting. "Shh, Mina. Don't share it with anybody. We have more enemies than friends here, she sighed. For years, we have been stuck in the western and extremist game. Since two hundred years ago, in this house, every day has been a celebration, a joy, and a party. People had enough freedom to enjoy life. They weren't afraid of each other. But now, we can't raise our voices, even in our own home because our land has become the playground of the western and extremists. Today, they invite our daughters to the West, and yesterday, the Taliban shot our daughters in the same city they hesitated to help. "Never mind," Mina said. "Why do you think like this, Mom? We need to be optimistic about the future."

"Because we are the victims of a game of chess. Before, our land was in the hands of extremists, now it is in the hands of the U.S., and tomorrow, who knows who we will be the next player."

Mom stretched out her legs, rubbed her swollen knee from arthritis with a eucalyptus pomade. The sharp smell filled the room as she said, "Afghans are simple-hearted and kind always, but we do not let the extremists make a nest here." Mom gave the pomade to Mina and asked her to rub her back. "This pain is going to kill me." While Mina rubbed her shoulder and back, her mom continued, "I don't know why anyone who is angry with his country around the world converts to an extremist and comes to Afghanistan for the violence. Go, my darling. I am not against your trip; this country will not be fixed until people become educated. You are working for education; it is your job. Go. Don't pay attention to political players. You will learn the lesson from traveling that you won't learn in any other school. But you must be very careful. Go to sleep now. We will talk about it tomorrow."

Watch, handbag, cell phone, shoes. Forms completed and passport placed on the security table of the U.S embassy in Kabul. Mina stood still while a female officer patted down her shoulders and chest. "An invitation to the U.S., huh? Congratulations! Who invited you?" the officer asked. Mina did not answer; she was too worried her voice would quake. From behind her, another female officer said, "Her business does not concern you. Just do your job."

She put on her shoes, grabbed her bags from the scanning machine, and looked at the two officers. After a moment, she smiled at them. Then, she passed through security and walked to another building where she sat on a wooden chair in front of the entryway. After a few minutes, she heard her name in English and stepped toward the window. When it opened, the smell of strong coffee blew into her face. A large mug with the American flag on it sat on the other side of the window. An aged man with gray hair in a dark blue suit examined every paper in her file while sipping his coffee.

"I see that you are a good English speaker," he said.

"Yes, I can speak English."

"What is the reason you are invited to the U.S.?"

"As a student for training."

He paused and smiled. "You've been issued a diplomatic visa because powerful people support your program. This is a difficult visa to get. Do you understand that?" He scanned her face for an answer and nodded. "Please place your thumb on the scanner."

On the way home from Kabul, she looked at her passport and put it back in her bag again. She suddenly felt seized in panic. She could not do this. It would be impossible to leave Kandahar even for a few weeks, she thought. What would happen when she returned from America? What would happen to her students in prison while she was gone?

The thought of Haroon—his darkened eyes, wounded face, and tobacco smell—attacked her mind yet again. What would he do if he knew she was thinking of leaving? Her body stiffened. She looked outside the window of the bus. The messy copper color of the sunset reflected on the brown and gray mountains. The sheep wranglers looked like tiny white dots on the desert's chest, and the fires next to the gypsy tents gleamed like orange spots in the desert's eye. The broken signs next to the road flew by her eyes. *Kandahar 100 miles*, the sign said. *100 miles to the Taliban*, she thought.

When she arrived home, her mother had cleaned and rinsed the dust from the cement in the yard and set a kettle of green tea on the table next to the garden. The fragrance from the flowers mixed with the wet dust and made a peaceful aroma that reminded her of childhood. She removed her burqa and sat on the old rug. She gave her passport to her mother.

Her mother turned the pages, her eye catching on the visa. She smiled with sad eyes. Her hands started shaking, and she set the passport down. She inhaled and smiled with her mouth. "I knew that everything would go well for you. It is time for you to think about leaving Kandahar."

Mina did not ask if she meant for the three-week training trip—or forever. She wasn't sure she could handle the answer. "But what will happen if I leave?" she asked.

"Nothing will happen, dear. The sun will rise and fall like always." Her eyes were wet and glossy as she looked at the teapot.

"I am being serious, Mother. What will Haroon do if I leave Kandahar?"

"Do you care what that stupid man does? Do what you want to do. He has the power over the city nowadays, but he does not have the power to stop you."

"But—" Mina said.

Her mother interrupted, "I wished you would take another path in your life, a path with less danger and difficulty. But it is your life, and you must not stop yourself. Don't worry about us. He cannot do anything to us."

Her mother still did not look at her. Mina knew her mother cried on the inside, and the dent on her forehead would deepen.

Her mother sat up straight and rolled up her sleeves. She tucked her long, gray hair under her scarf. She began to pray quietly as she moved her hands under the water pipe. Her tears mixed with the water as she wiped her face. She let the water drip down her chin. Then she looked at the sky, dried her face with her scarf, and began whispering so quietly that Mina could not understand.

Dear Erick,

I can't believe it—I passed my test, and I get to go to the U.S. for leadership training! This is an amazing opportunity, and I am so excited. I am also scared to leave Kandahar for many reasons. I just wanted to say thank you for encouraging me and supporting me with the different supplies you have sent. It is very helpful to have a friend who is looking out for me, my mother, and our students, who understands our life here, and who helps us through difficult times. I will let you know how my training goes.

Thank you again,
Mina

Dear Mina,

Congratulations! I am so proud of you. I look forward to hearing all about it!

Sincerely,
Erick

Chapter 10

Dead Swallows

I t was early in the morning. The sky was still dark, and in the past, birds would have been singing in the willow trees around the house. But Mina hadn't heard the bird's song since her childhood. With each explosion and resulting fire, hundreds of swallows had fallen from the branches of the surrounding trees. She used to run into the valley to pick up the birds and drip a drop of water into their beaks to try to save their lives, but it was hopeless. The birds were already dead from fear. She did not know why she was thinking of the dead swallows again on the day of her departure.

She locked her suitcase and looked at her shoes; they were the shoes she had bought with her close friend, Sanam. These shoes were saviors. They identified her as a different person anytime she covered herself with her burqa and left her home.

She remembered the New Year's Eve when Sanam stayed overnight, and mother brought the old copper bowl from the basement and threw the green henna powder into it. Sanam and Mina both watched the henna powder with their curious eyes, and her mother yelled, "Pour the water!" Mina gradually added a jug of water to the bowl of henna powder, and her mother prepared the henna powder into a green paste. How did dark green paste turn red on her fingers? She always asked herself.

"Girls, give me your hands." Mother would paint the henna paste to the delicate fingers of Sanam and Mina, then tie them with golden cotton handkerchiefs. She used to say that the golden-green handkerchiefs belonged to her wedding ceremony when Grandma put henna on her hands on her wedding night! Sanam's big smile made the holes on her cheeks deeper and her big eyes brighter. Mina's room was filled with the smell of fresh henna on New Year nights.

When they slept, they put their bandaged hands on their chests so that they would not make a mistake and move in bed because the henna patterns on their fingertips would be ruined. They should sleep with henna on their hands until morning. Mother said that the color of henna works better at night. The girls put their hands on their chests and laughed and moved like the motionless dead.

Sometimes Sanam put her hands on her mouth as if she were laughing. Mina shouted, "Do not shake those stupid hands of yours!" On the Morning of Eid, the smell of dry henna engulfed their lungs and the two of them opened their palms happily. The red color of Henna played across their fingertips like beautiful Kandahar pomegranate flowers blossoming on their soft skin.

She didn't like to think about Sanam. The last time she'd seen her, her purple face had been hanging from her bedroom ceiling. Mina wiped tears from her eyes as she cleaned her shoes. She wished Sanam hadn't been forced to marry against her will, forced to hang herself or live in misery. If she were alive now, perhaps she and Mina would hug and find things to laugh about like they always did. She pulled her bag to the red rug in the hallway. The rug brought her mind to the nights of bombardment, when all the neighbors came to their house to sit on the red rug. One of the neighbor children's faces turned colorless in her mom's arms as she held her there on the rug. Blood ran down, and the rug absorbed it. Mother had washed the red rug after that night, but still, she could see the small pale face and the little bloody body in the woven flowers.

She couldn't control the unwanted thoughts; they attacked her mind when she left the house.

"Do not wear the new shoes; wear the old, ugly ones so you look like an old woman," her mother said. Then she whispered, "Do not take off your burqa at the airport." With tears on her cheeks, she gave Mina her old burqa. "Go now, go!"

Father was waiting for her at the door. "Don't worry, my girl, everything will be okay," he said. He kissed her forehead. "I cannot come with you to the airport; someone might recognize me and create a problem for you. I want everything to go smoothly for you today." Mina hugged him hard.

As she walked away with her bag, she heard the door close behind her. Tears rolled from her face and onto her arms.

An old, rusted bus with reed-covered seats headed to the Kandahar airport on a road outside the city. They drove through a cloud of black smoke that filled the inside of the bus. The smell of gasoline made her gag; she looked around to see others gagging, too. Her mouth felt like someone else had spit in her mouth. A headache blossomed and squeezed her temples.

The bus ran over a rock, causing her head to knock against the window. Suddenly, the bus lost control and slid into the dirt next to the road. Everything was chaotic and blurry—tangled together. Her ears rang from the inside like someone blew a horn in her ears. She could not hear anything, and when people started jumping from the bus, she could not move.

A woman sitting behind her began pulling her hair and screaming. Children were crying. Pieces of the broken window were buried in Mina's hands. The smell of burned rubber and human hair filled her nostrils. She saw the black smoke as it rose to the clear blue sky. The road was filled with burning objects. The Americans, with their khaki tanks and soldiers, ran into the smoke. A soldier held his hand up to say stop in front of the other cars. The tanks had closed the roads and helicopters filled the sky above. Through the haze, her eye caught two soldiers running toward the bus. She heard in English, "No one is hurt."

A local interpreter with a dusty face covered by a black and white scarf yelled, "Go! Go! Take the back road! This road is now closed!" Mina knew then that she would miss her flight.

"What happened?" a passenger asked the interpreter.

"Landmine," he replied. "Two Americans were killed. No one else."

What if one of those soldiers is Erick? Mina thought, then shook her head. It couldn't be him—this man she had never met. He left over a year ago...but what if it was him? Soldiers always got killed. Maybe Erick was sent to another war or another city? He could be dead now, or he could be anywhere. She would never know, but his kindness had stayed in the forefront of her mind.

Mina had grown up in war; she knew what it really was. Her definition of war was, "Nothing is special to war. War takes whoever it wants." She still hoped the bloody body being taken through the sky in the helicopter wasn't Erick's.

She turned on her phone—zero bars. The driver got back in the bus, still heading to the airport. Kids were crying, tears mixing with snot as they got back on the road. The wind rushing through the broken window somehow soothed her.

"Are you traveling alone?" The security officer asked while leafing through the pages of her passport at the airport.

"No, I'm with my uncle." She looked behind her.

The officer pounded the passport hard on the table. "You think I'm stupid?" He continued flipping through her pages. "I see you are going to Dubai first. How many days will you stay in Dubai?"

"Only a few hours. I am waiting in the airport for my next flight."

"Really? I know young, pretty girls like you can have a good income in Dubai." The officer looked at his watch and threw the passport on the table. "Go."

Eyes followed her in unsaid communication: *What are you doing here alone?* The airport cleaner hit her leg with his broom. "Are you blind? Get out of here! Go sit in the women's area!" She wanted to slap the boy in the face, and the customs officer, too. But she said nothing and slid over to the women's area, crumpling herself under her burqa.

Just then, she noticed him; she saw the ugly scar on his face. He had found her. He gave money to the cleaner and whispered something in his ear. Mina shrunk down even more inside her burqa and tried to hide among the other women around her. She always asked herself, *Why must we women of Kandahar hide ourselves with a burqa?* Now she was so happy to be wearing one. She breathed deeply, knowing there would always be a man looking to kill, hurt, or kidnap her and all the other women. Her burqa still smelled like her mother. She kissed the inside of it as Haroon walked past her.

He was only inches away when the speakers in the airport announced her flight for check-in. As she stood, the corner of her burqa got tangled in another passenger's luggage. Suddenly, she was stuck. She felt the terrible man pull on the back of her burqa. She twisted free and felt her heart pound in her chest.

There is no way he can stop me now, she thought once she was inside the plane. No country would let him in with his violent history. But she knew he was like poisoned air that seeped everywhere unseen. What will I do if he follows me? She felt her breath catch in fear. She buckled her seatbelt and took out her phone to call home but didn't know what to say. She finally texted her parents,

I'm almost departing. Love you both. Bye.

Chapter 11

Blood on Blankets

*T*he airplane was cold. Mina had taken off her burqa, finally; she was allowed to because it was not a domestic flight. It had been a relief to breathe freely, but now she felt vulnerable and wished she was still wearing it. She tore open the plastic bag on her seat with her teeth and pulled out a dark blue blanket that smelled like a hospital. She covered herself and pressed against the window, then closed her eyes.

Haroon had been in the line. It was him; she knew it. He had followed her so many times on her way home from prison, the bazaar, the mausoleum, her friend's home, and now he still followed her, even outside of Kandahar. In her dream, many other men also followed her in dark, cold, foggy air. All of them had eyes rimmed in kohl and faces blurred by fog. She saw herself inside a coffin. She heard the *tic tic* sound of rain hitting the lid, yet she could not move her body. She knew she would soon feel the wet soil on her face, in her ears and her eyes, covering her hair and body. Inside the coffin, she heard more noises.

Men carried her coffin until the terrible man snapped his fingers, signaling to them to put it down. Then, he sat next to her, took out a knife, and put it on her throat. Mina could not feel anything, yet she heard the knife tearing apart the vessels in her neck. Her blood poured all over his face as he cleaned the knife on his sleeve. By the light of the fire, she saw the outline of the scars on his happy face. His eyes were laughing. As the blood dried on her chest and arms, he dragged her headless body to the fire. The blue and red flames rose all the way to the sky and began to consume her. Still, she felt nothing.

When she opened her eyes, she saw a mass of clouds mixing with the color of the sun. The spectrum of light from the sunset was fabulous. Her eyes soared like a bird around the endless, silent sky.

More than at any time before, she felt lonely on the plane. There was no longer distance in her mind between reality and dreams as she floated among the clouds. The repeated nightmares about the terrible man were never far from her; she never knew when they were coming.

She suddenly had a terrible headache. As she drowned in her thoughts, she noticed droplets of blood on the airplane window. She didn't know where they were from, but she wiped the blood on the blanket. When she looked down, a shower of fevered blood burbled from her nose.

The man sitting next to her jumped up and shouted, "Nurse, Nurse! Help, here!"

The nurse arrived quickly, wearing a yellow vest over her blue uniform. "What happened?" she asked.

"I don't know. I'm alright, it's just..." She could not say anymore.

The bloody cotton swabs filled the shiny nurse's table. She smelled the alcohol, and a sharp pain rushed inside her brain. When the nurse left her, she held her back straight and her head back looking at the tiny blinking stars on the curved ceiling of the plane. Somehow, those artificial stars made her feel better as the salty taste of blood filled her throat. A strange heat was burning her inside. When she touched the monitor in front of her, it said, "Place: Greenland. Temperature: -30° centigrade."

The man sitting next to her was staring at her. She stood to go to the restroom but did not want to look in the mirror; she didn't want to see herself. She washed her face, and the water made her forehead calm and cold. She took off her shirt and cleaned the dried blood from her neck. She put the bloody shirt inside her bag and picked up a clean gray shirt, but when she glanced in the small mirror, her heart dropped. Haroon stood right behind her. He looked like he was going to swallow her naked body. She put her hands on her breasts and opened her mouth to scream, but then stopped and steeled herself. She threw the shirt on and pushed the bloody tissues into the trash. She pushed her thoughts of the evil man in there, too, with all her might. She felt better when she returned to her seat.

Chapter 12

The Sad Face of Christ

Rebecca held a piece of paper with Mina's name on it in large letters at the exit of the baggage claim. When Mina recognized her name and approached her, they hugged. Rebecca smiled and took her luggage.

"It's so nice to finally meet you in person!" Rebecca said.

Mina smiled, "Thank you for inviting me."

"Did you get some rest on the flight?"

She nodded.

"We are going to my house to rest and prepare; the program starts on Monday," Rebecca said as she closed the trunk with her bags. "I hope you don't mind staying with me, but if you feel like you would be more comfortable with the other women in the program, we can change it. What do you think?"

Mina smiled and said, "I would love to stay with an empowered woman like you. This is an amazing opportunity. Thank you so much."

Rebecca smiled, "Perfect, let's go!"

Rebecca stopped at a red light, and Mina looked out, stunned by the beauty of the buildings in downtown Washington D.C. She rolled down the car window and a new smell hit her face, but she barely noticed. It was Saturday, and the sidewalks were filled with young women enjoying their time with their loved ones as they strolled shoulder to shoulder, hand in hand, or walked alone with their pets. Mina didn't hear what else Rebecca had said. She saw her red lips moving, but all she could hear were the sounds of the women outside. It was still impossible for her to grasp how different it was from Kandahar. *Those women must not be real*, she thought. *Their freedom is greater than that of the whole world combined.*

Memories of her grandmother came to mind. She had peppered her with questions when she was little, "Why must women in Kandahar cover themselves head to toe in burqas? Did God tell them to do that? But God is the same for all women, isn't he? Then why don't women on TV or in movies cover themselves from head to toe like our women?"

"You are so little, but you already know how to open old wounds and pour salt on them," she had said. She took Mina's hand inside of her wrinkled hands. "No, darling, God never said to put women under a moving cage, and yes, God is the same for all women. Someday, you will understand."

Mina's eyes locked on the street, but her mind was replaying her grandmother's words. She wondered how the extremists tricked everyone into believing God wanted women in cages and men to blow themselves up. She was baffled. Why do people agree to live, or in many cases, die, like this?

The car stopped in front of a large house made of red brick with huge, white windows. An expansive lawn dazzled in front of her with bright flowers filling the corners of the garden and the areas under the windows.

Rebecca opened the front door, then put her purse and keys on a hutch in the hallway. "Come upstairs with me. I'll show you your room."

They walked into a big room decorated with scented candles and beautiful flowers in blue vases around a cheerful bed with a red and cream duvet and cream-colored curtains.

"I'm going to make dinner now, and Matt will be home soon. You'll like my husband Matt—he's a doctor."

Later, as Mina sat alone in the dining room, she stared at the large cross made of stone on the wall behind Rebecca's seat. Two tall candles blinked on either side of the cross, casting a shadow on the wall behind Jesus's body as it hung from the cross. All the lights in the dining room were dim, and Christ's sad face looked pure and saintly.

The front door opened, and she heard a young, deep voice, "Hello?" Rebecca spoke to the voice in a low murmur she couldn't hear.

Rebecca walked in a few minutes later with a tray full of steak, mashed potatoes, asparagus, bread rolls, and butter, which she put in the center of the table. Soon after, a man with a shaved face and sharp, gray eyes in a dark blue shirt came into the living room.

"Mina, this is Matt. Matt, this is Mina," Rebecca said as he reached out his hand and shook hers.

Rebecca talked about the traffic from the airport and the busy day she'd had before then. Matt shook his head and chewed his food quietly, looking like his mind was somewhere else.

After half a glass of red wine, Matt leaned back in his chair, and while he cleaned his mouth gently with a light blue, cloth napkin, he pulled up his sleeves and calmly said, "You had a long trip, Mina. How was your flight? His gray eyes were shining, but behind his eyes was an unknown feeling that Mina couldn't understand. His eyes locked on Mina like he'd found a new patient in his office and wanted to check out everything.

Mina said, "Yes, it was a long flight, and it was good."

"I do not have any idea what is going on in the Middle East. We do not hear any good news from those countries except violence. Right?" Then he picked up the glass and shook it. The ice pieces hit the glass and broke the silence. He looked at Mina and spoke, "Is it true that the Afghans are always killing each other?"

Mashed potatoes stuck in Mina's throat like a fish bone. She drank the whole glass of water to wash it down.

Rebecca hit Matt's arm with her elbow. "Mina don't answer that. Matt, why don't you tell us about your day?"

"No, seriously, why must the Afghans always kill each other? When will it stop?"

"Matt," Rebecca interrupted, "did you know Mina is giving a speech tomorrow? She needs to get some rest. Right, Mina?"

Mina nodded, her eyes suddenly blurry with fatigue and sadness.

When she was back in her room, she could hardly breathe, not because of the scented candles and warm room temperature, but because she felt like she was suffocating. She needed fresh air.

As she opened the windows, she felt the wind hit her face and blow her hair back. She kicked herself a thousand times for not answering Matt at the dinner table. Why would she get quiet when it was most important to speak? The wind refreshed her but did not stop her self-loathing. Matt's questions had hit her brain so quickly she froze. She wished she would have said, *"Look, Matt, war is war. It is like when a disease comes into a body, it will affect the entire body. It is like cancer. Do you have any patients with cancer? Cells kill and consume each other because of the diseased state. Disease and war are the same. In Afghanistan, we have been fighting the disease of war for four decades. So, the better question is, what or who caused the disease? Throughout the history of Afghanistan, who introduced the problems?"* But she had said nothing; she'd only bit her lips and reminded herself that the people of Afghanistan were cursed, not just to live and die at the hands of extremists in their own land, but in how the world perceived them.

Chapter 13

Woman in Fire

Enormous chandeliers hung from the ceiling of the National Women's Museum; yellow lights reflected on the revolving white staircases. The unfamiliar sights and sparkling crystals of the hanging fixtures hypnotized. Mina felt tired as she ascended the stairs. She noticed a familiar smell, but she couldn't place it. When had she smelled it before? And where?

The portraits of women on the walls caught her eyes; she could not stop staring at them. A small light was attached to the top of each frame, illuminating each picture, and setting it apart from its surroundings. There was a pale lady with skinny, whitish lips and tired eyes in one of the paintings. The high, purple collar of her dress held her long neck like a fragile vase. Mina noticed a band of mysterious colors in the background; it looked like dried flowers or a garden on a fire. Suddenly, Mina knew exactly what, or who, it was. There was a man standing behind the woman. His face appeared from the colors—blue, purple, dark blue, and black. His kohl-rimmed eyes were like charcoal on fire seen from centuries away. She felt like he was stroking her and the lady's neck, too. She ran downstairs to take a huge gulp of fresh air. Had he found her again?

"Where were you?" Rebecca asked. "You disappeared. Come on, we need to hurry. It's your time to talk, and I want you to meet the director." She took Mina's hand. "Don't be nervous."

The director of the Women's Empowerment Organization projected a deep sense of calm. Clean makeup and a pearl necklace covered the wrinkles on her face and neck, her blond hair was bobbed, and her bangs were cut short and straight. She wore a blue suit with a golden pin on the lapel. The women around her looked interested to meet Mina. One of them said, "Our organization has been supporting women like you around the world who want to help make their country a better place for women. We are so happy to have you as our special guest here." Mina wasn't sure how to respond; she was still nervous from the episode at the painting.

On stage, Mina wanted to talk about her work for female prisoners and the future programs she wanted to help create for women, but she forgot the words she had rehearsed. She wanted to speak about the issues that she was reminded of throughout every day, but she couldn't. Instead, she said, "Hello, everyone, my name is Mina. I have come from a land where all the women have been forgotten. It has been years that we have been hidden behind an invisible fence that stops us from living the life we want, a fence called fanaticism. The other invisible fence is the one we wear, the burqa. These two fences can jail our bodies, but they cannot jail our spirits. We have lost our freedom, but we will not lose our faith or our hope. We will work every day to regain our lost freedom, so our children can know a different way. So, they can know life with freedom instead of fanaticism."

After she stepped down from the stage, Rebecca laid her head on Mina's shoulder. She held up her phone and took a selfie. "Smile!" she said, and then asked, "Why are you so serious? I can see the creases on your forehead. It's okay, Mina, you did great!"

When they got back into the house, Rebecca took a shower. Moments later, she ran into Mina's room in her towel, her shoulders still wet, screaming in excitement. "Mina, a TV program will be here tomorrow to interview you about your work in Afghanistan!"

Mina was shocked, but she tried to hide it.

"Why the long face; are you not happy about this? Are you nervous?"

"Journalists always make everything so dramatic, Rebecca. I don't want to be interviewed."

"Mina, you will do fine. You were great today. Don't worry!" Rebecca sat down on Mina's bed in her towel and crossed her legs. She held her coffee in one hand and scrolled on her phone with the other, looking through the pictures she had taken with Mina.

"Can I call my parents?" Mina asked her.

"Sure," Rebecca said without looking up from her phone. It was nighttime in D.C., but daytime in Kandahar, and her mother was a morning person. Mina waited a few moments for her mom to answer.

"Hello?"

"Mama, it's me."

"Mina, where are you? Is everything okay?"

"Everything's fine, Mama. I am still in Washington DC. I am leaving here soon to come home, but I'm worried about you and Dad. Are you okay?"

"We are fine, Mina. There's no need to worry about us."

"Okay, good. I want to buy you something. Do you need anything?"

"Forget the gifts. We don't need anything," her mom said. Then, her voice got softer. "Listen, Kandahar is a small town, you know, and this trip of yours to America—everyone in the city knows about it. Yesterday, a policeman asked your father about you; he came from the prison. I don't think you should come back so soon; stay a little longer if you can. Take more time away from that terrible man who is waiting for you. Don't worry, you won't lose your job. And if you do, you can get a better job later. Do you understand? Stay there for a while."

Mina didn't respond.

"Hello, Mina? Hello? Are you there?"

Mina hung up and sat in a chair against the wall, sweating. She dropped her head into her hands.

Rebecca came to her and put her hand on her shoulder. "Hey, what happened? Are you okay?"

"I'm fine. I'm just tired," Mina said. She stood and opened the patio door. It was almost the last day of spring. There was a light rain; blossoms from the cherry trees fluttered to the ground. The cool air felt fresh on her face. She had a decision to make.

The next morning, Rebecca combed her short blond hair with her fingers in the hallway mirror. She wore red lipstick, a short white skirt, and high-heeled black shoes. "I want to show you my old office, Mina. Let's go."

She parked her car in front of an older building. There were stone statues posing in front of all the buildings downtown that all looked angry to Mina. Mina could smell the rich scent of coffee as she and Rebecca walked up the circular staircase. "I spoke to my old boss from when I was a journalist. He is very interested in meeting you. I want you to see the office of my previous newsroom, too."

Mina sat on a yellow couch in the waiting room while Rebecca knocked on the door jam and walked into her old boss's office. The walls of the waiting room were covered with pictures of elephants and donkeys wearing suits. One picture showed them shaking hands, another showed them back-to-back, angry.

Rebecca poked her head out of the office, "Mina, come here, please."

Her ex-boss was named Paul. He was an old man with a hunched back and a black, striped shirt. He stood up from his chair and squeezed Mina's hand with his big hands, then the three of them sat.

"Where are you from?" Paul asked Mina. He reminded her of a teacher.

"From Kandahar, Afghanistan."

Paul's eyes opened wide. "What a coincidence! I just received a message from my news reporters near there a couple of minutes ago. Unfortunately, some of our soldiers died near your city today." He looked at Mina for a few seconds. Mina felt like he wanted her to tell him the reason for their deaths. "The town was called Maiwand. Would you show me that on the map, please?" He pointed to the huge map of Afghanistan on his wall.

She stood up and put her finger on a tiny black dot. "Here's Maiwand, south of Kandahar."

Paul looked at the map and then at her. "Do you think the lives our soldiers have lost there have improved your lives at all?" he asked.

Mina swallowed and looked at Paul nervously. She did not know if there was a correct answer to his question; she only knew her truth. "The reason why I am here today is because of your soldiers. I did not go to school until I was fifteen because of the Taliban. I was jailed at home until then. Do you know why? Because I am a woman. I do not know much about politics, but I do know that there are thousands of other girls like me who are able to go to school and prepare for higher education—only because of your soldiers."

Paul got up from his chair. He walked to the corner of his office and took a small American flag. He walked toward Mina and said quietly, "The reason I work behind my desk with a peaceful mind is because of our soldiers, too." With a sad smile, he gave the flag to Mina. "Here is a gift for you."

Rebecca took a deep breath. "I think it's time for us to leave now."

Mina smiled and nodded her head at Paul, then put the flag carefully in her purse. She spent the rest of her trip attending meetings with Rebecca and speaking at several events about her life in Kandahar. On the last day, she finished packing and said goodbye to the pretty bedroom she had grown comfortable in. She met Rebecca at the bottom of the stairs, her eyes smiling and shiny.

"Three weeks went by very fast, Mina. I'm so glad you stayed with us. You will be an amazing role model. I hope I see you back here for more training soon."

Chapter 14

Dizziness

Mina bought some perfume and a box of chocolate at the airport. The shopping distracted her from the worry that crept into her head. There was not much time left before her flight, and she knew she had to be on it. There was no other way. But stepping onto the plane felt like stepping into the hands of death, impossible to escape. She did not mind the idea of dying because a significant part of her felt disgraceful. But at the hands of Haroon? No. She could not allow this to happen. But she did not know how to avoid it; she had to go home.

"Flight 1724 from Washington to Dubai now checking in at gate ten."

As she stood to board her flight, her vision went dark. She could see only shadows as she pulled her bag onto her shoulder. She felt like a comet was heading straight for her, floating in space, while waiting in line behind the other passengers—ticket, and passport in hand. Suddenly, she knew she would vomit. There was only one person left in front of her to scan her passport and enter the plane. *Please no! Please no!* she said to herself, but she couldn't wait. She ran to the bathroom and threw up. She sat on the floor of the stall and tried to catch her breath and feel well enough to stand. Her head was spinning, and her vision shook. She had to close her eyes. She wasn't sure how long she sat like that, but when she could finally stand and walk out to the gate, she saw that it had been hours. She had missed her flight.

She squeezed her eyes shut, feeling more confused than she had ever been, and more unsure about right from wrong, living from dying, and day from night. Her mind was like a ball of string tightly wound together in meaning but slowly unraveling from the other end.

She sat at an empty gate for hours, not knowing what to do. This was not the first time she had vomited from fear and lost time. She could not collect herself. She thought about calling Rebecca, but what would she say? She could not disappoint her after all she had done for her. *But maybe this is a sign,* she thought. *I shouldn't go home. I'm not meant to die yet. My work in this world is not done.*

Erick came to her mind. He had been kind and generous to her, sending supplies for her and the students, checking in—and he knew Kandahar. He knew what she had lived through and what awaited her return. She quickly opened her bag and took out her laptop. She saw her mom's burqa and stared at it for a minute, then touched it and tucked it down further. She turned on her laptop. Erick felt like her only hope of salvation, but she had never met him in person and did not know where he lived. She only knew it was somewhere in this enormous country. Was this crazy? Yes, it was crazy. She closed her laptop and slid it into her bag.

She walked around the airport shops until midnight, stopping in front of jewelry stores for no reason other than the sparkle. She saw a man buy a gold ring with a huge smile. He put the ring in a little red box and then put it in the pocket of his jacket. Mina imagined the woman getting that ring would jump up and down like a child getting a new toy. This made her momentarily happy.

She went to a bookstore and flipped through the pages of a newspaper. She saw a picture on the cover of a magazine of an American movie star she had seen in some movies. "How To Look Skinny," it said. Then, "10 Ways to Grow Sexual Desire in Women," and, "10 Ways to Look Younger." She wished she had these trivial concerns.

Her eyes were stinging; she knew she had a fever. She bought a cup of coffee, but the taste was more bitter than usual. In a different restaurant, she bought a bottle of water. It was past midnight when she turned on her laptop again. She had to send another email, but she did not know where to start or what to say.

> Hello Erick,
>
> I have just finished my training program in the U.S. I have no idea if you are in the United States or not, but I'm not quite ready to go home. If you are here, is it possible for you to have a guest for a few days?
>
> With all respect,
>
> Mina

She waited for Erick's response as she watched people coming and going throughout the night. The people stepping off planes looked insanely tired. The people leaving were insanely glad. She wasn't sure in which group she belonged. She prayed in whispers to get out of this painful moment. It was close to 2 a.m. when she checked her email again. She'd never been so happy to see a name.

> Hello Mina,

I'm so happy you completed your training in America. I live in Northern California now. I bought you a ticket (I hope you don't mind; I had all your information from when you sent it to me so you could receive the supplies) and have attached it to this email. I'll be at the San Francisco airport waiting for you. See you soon.

—Erick

Mina's shoulders dropped. She felt like she had just escaped a dark and deep hole. She had walked the airport throughout the night, and now the sunrise reflected on the windows. She felt empty inside, but at the same time, she was full of energy. She pulled out a small hand mirror and looked at her dried lips. Her eyes were red from not sleeping. She looked as ill as she felt. As she waited for the flight to San Francisco, she thought of an earlier email Erick had sent to her.

Leaving Kandahar was a sad moment for me. I had hoped to get back again, but it did not happen. The students there are so eager to learn and so appreciative of every opportunity to do so, no matter how small. Never could I have imagined knowing a teacher from Kandahar. I believe I belong to that city somehow.

—Erick

Remembering Erick's words made her feel better. Finally, she made her way inside the plane. She sat next to a man wearing white headphones; he twirled the cord around his finger. Three silver chains hung from holes in one of his ears. She scooted past him and sat in the window seat.

The man took off his headphones. "I'm sure San Francisco is going to be interesting to you," he said. He sipped his drink and looked at her with ocean blue eyes. "Most visitors to our city are either artists or businesspeople. Let me guess, which one are you? Not a business lady...either an artist, dancer, musician, designer, singer, or...?"

She didn't know what to say. She thought of saying, *Escaping is an art, too,* because there was something in escaping that cannot be found in any other art. Escaping was like creating something out of nothing in a different time and a different place.

When the man saw that she wasn't responding, his smile disappeared. He distracted himself with his drink.

She didn't know why his question bothered her. She thought of her teenage years during the Taliban regime, when she often thought about escaping. Before then, she hadn't known why her parents worried so much about her becoming a woman.

When autumn arrived in Kandahar with its glorious colors among tangled mountains, cold winds whistled through the hills. Hindukush's mountains were covered in white, and the pomegranate trees shed their leaves. But that year, the drought had turned the wind into a two-headed snake. The head with the brains agonized in pain. The other head had eyes and nose as red as the core of fire.

Every evening, sandstorms approached Kandahar. No one could see anything. One night, as Mina was out in the yard, sand ground between her teeth as the wind brought notes from a symphony of horror through the windows. A lightning bolt broke the sky apart and made a beast's sound a few moments later.

Dark gray clouds strangled each other, but one droplet of rain did not drop. Yellow scorpions left their place from the ground. It was like they already knew something strange would happen.

"I have never seen a drought so bad as this," her father said.

The area under Mother's eyes went darker and deeper every day. "What is this tragedy happening in our city?" she asked her husband.

"The Taliban. Like hungry grasshoppers, they swarm the city from four sides. Everything that comes in their way, they destroy."

"Where is the Taliban from?" Mina asked.

Father ripped the dried grape tree roots out of the garden. "I have no idea where the hell they are from. They have fought for many years; they fought against The Soviets, and now they think that to build the country, they must fight against the women."

This was the first time she'd heard about men who dressed in black and darkened their eyes and targeted women.

She remembered the morning when she had woken up and dressed for school as usual. She went to the kitchen and saw her mother's pale face, her pajamas still on.

"Why are you not getting ready yet? Are you sick, or are all the teachers off?" Mina asked her, but she didn't respond. Her eyes reflected the teacup on the table. Mina went to her father, sitting in the corner of the garden with a bitter smile.

"From this day on, you, your mother, and the other girls in Kandahar are not going to school or leaving our home. They closed all the girls' schools," he said, laying his hand on Mina's cheek. "But please don't worry, my girl. I will buy you many books so you can study just as hard."

Mina felt like a bucket of cold water had been thrown on her head.

At night, only the sounds of crickets and gun fire could be heard. Shot after shot, and round after round of bullets. She heard a man yell, "Stop!" and then whimpers of pain.

One night, she awoke to see her father removing the living room rug and digging a hole under it by the light of an oil lamp.

"War is war. Nothing matters," he mumbled. He pulled out a hunting caliber gun from the hole where he'd hid it earlier, unrolling the dusty cotton from around it. "The Taliban are kidnapping girls from our neighborhood, and they are waiting for our daughter," he said as he cleaned the gun. He aimed the gun at the ground. "No man will trespass against my young daughter while I am alive." He then hid the gun in the closet.

Her parents were filling up the hole while Mina's heart was emptying. It was like all her happiness was being buried in that same hole. She thought she must be very grown up now to have so many worries in her heart.

That night, she stood in front of the mirror in her room, naked. Her body was long and slim, her hair dark and shiny. The two masses on her chest made her uncomfortable. It hadn't been that long before that she was shaped like a boy. She used to dress up like a boy to enjoy some freedom. Could she still, with this new body? She would try.

She hid her hair under her hat. She put on pants and a jacket of her father's and snuck out of the house. She went straight to her favorite place: the bookstore. But it was nothing like the place it had been. Where her favorite books had been—right up front—were now gasoline containers and cigarette bags. The smell of papers and new books was gone, replaced by fumes from leaking oil containers. Even the librarian was gone. The man in the shop stared at her like she owed him money. She walked down the aisle, her back hunched to hide her body.

As she approached the door to leave, the man pulled her back and then hit her leg with a wooden stick. "Ay! Thief boy! Where are you going? Hurry up and show me what you're hiding in your shirt!"

She pushed him to the side and ran the whole way home.

Back then, Mina and the other girls in the neighborhood would sit under a grape tree with yellow leaves in her garden.

Mother would bring them green tea and dried fruits and teach their lessons there. Once, on a Friday, she played a recording from a Mulla. His lesson of the day was about women.

"Women are dirty! We mustn't get too close to them when they are on their menstrual cycle. We mustn't eat food from their hands. After a woman has a baby, they are nasty for forty days. Don't look at their face in the morning; it will bring you bad luck. Fathers, be smart. When your girls are mature, give them away to a husband."

Mother said, "Be quiet or the Mulla will kick you out of your house as though you have your period." The girls laughed.

Her father came out of the house, his face red with anger. "Shame on you!" he said. He made Mother bring them inside and close the windows.

Mother taught the girls how to dance and make music on the drum with their fingers. The girls circled and moved faster and faster, dancing. The air in their skirts made them feel lighter, like they were flying like birds. They soared and danced, moving, and spinning around and around, releasing themselves from the traps the Mulla made for them.

The noise of the people exiting woke her from her daydream. The plane had landed. She stood and took her bag from above. The man beside her nodded with a smile. "Welcome to San Francisco."

Chapter 15

Ocean Breeze

A tall man with gray shorts and a navy t-shirt walked toward her from the crowd. She did not think it was Erick, though she had never seen him. She assumed from the way he had worded his emails that he must be an older man, maybe older than her father. But Erick was young and attractive, maybe her own age. He held out his hand and shook hers. "I'm Erick," he said. She took a deep breath when he said his name.

It was an afternoon in June. She could smell the ocean past the wooden fence of his backyard. She stood under an old palm tree looking at hummingbirds flitting from tree to tree, their wings buzzing. When she stepped closer to them, they flew away. She admired the garden; it was lovely, filled with flowers and a lemon tree teeming with ripe lemons. Erick took her suitcases from the trunk, and she followed him inside to the living room. Her eyes went straight to the weights lined up from light to heavy close to the fireplace. The walls were filled with pictures of a little kid very similar to Erick. *Is it him in his childhood?* she wondered. It all looked simple and clean.

"Let me show you your room," Erick said. He turned on the lights and placed her bags on the fluffy, floral comforter, then

83

leaned against the frame of the door. It looked like he was going to say something, but he didn't. Instead, he turned and left her alone.

Mina was exhausted. She tumbled onto the bed with her shoes still on and fell into a deeper sleep than she'd had in years. She woke several hours later to the sound of knocking at her door. For a moment, she forgot where she was. She looked outside the window. She couldn't tell if it was morning or night. "Dinner is ready!" Erick said, and it all came back to her.

Although she had not eaten for an entire day, she still was not hungry. But she didn't want to be rude, so she ate a piece of chicken with sticky white rice. "I don't know how to cook; I just bought this food. I hope you like it." Erick said and then smiled. "The world is so small! I never thought I'd have a guest from Kandahar."

Mina automatically felt comfortable with Erick. He was so calm and friendly. It was the first time in her life she could sit and eat with a man alone without judgment, fear, or disrespect. It was hard for her to imagine, but it was true.

"It seems so quiet here. It doesn't sound like anyone lives in this city," Mina said.

Erick laughed. "We are in the suburbs of San Francisco; inside the city it is more crowded. If you miss the crowds, I'll take you to see San Francisco."

Mina smiled, "I would like that."

"You must be very tired. I'll clean up the table so you can go back to sleep."

But Mina wasn't tired, hungry, sad, or happy. She wasn't sure what she was. Suddenly, she knew she needed to be alone. She wanted to enjoy this moment without fears, worries, or bad feelings. She wanted to freeze time so she could remember this feeling forever. She wasn't sure she would still feel this way tomorrow.

She went to bed and closed her eyes again. She knew she was safe in Erick's house for the night, but her soul was agitated like a tumultuous sea. She thought of the day she first met Haroon. She got up, opened the window, and stuck her head outside. She breathed in the fresh air; she'd never smelled an ocean breeze before. But the terrible man was still there, like a dark wall in front of her.

Chapter 16

San Francisco

*T*he dive shop was dark and wet and smelled of mildew, like the basement of her home in Kandahar in the winter, when rain pushed the small windows open and raindrops found the corners, making the shelves damp. Huge dead fish hung on the wooden walls; hooks and ropes hung from every surface.

Erick's eyes were stuck on the dive lights, dive watches, knives, fins, air tanks; he was in his element, like a kid in a candy shop. "I need a new mask," he said. "I hope you don't mind. I don't get to the city very often."

Mina smiled. "Do you mind if I walk around the block by myself for a bit?"

Erick took off the mask. "Yes, of course. Let's meet at my car in twenty minutes. Do you remember where I parked?" Mina nodded.

"Don't get lost, okay?" he said, and Mina laughed.

Music echoed throughout the city, and Mina noticed people walking arm in arm, flushed with happiness. A couple in an outdoor restaurant sliced a piece of steak to share. They cracked the shell of a lobster and drank red wine. Everyone looked blissful to Mina.

Red lobsters cuddled each other in brown wooden barrels of water. It was as though they were planning an escape from the boiling water and hungry customers in their near future. Sea birds targeted pieces of bread to attack and feed on. Everything felt calm and safe.

Every time Mina walked down different blocks, the sights changed. On one block, people seemed to be thrown together from another world. Their hair was tangled and dirty; their clothes and bodies were the same color as the oily street. It looked like their faces had not been touched by water in years. They lived by garbage cans surrounded by broken bottles. Some of them curled around each other on the ground. The ones who seemed drunk lay on their sides like dry yellow leaves blown by the wind to the corner of the street. In the middle of a huge garbage area, some of them slept as though they had a silk pillow and the soft sheets of a king.

The trolley gave tourists a ride up and down the streets like a kid's wooden train. The old bell of the trolley rang. Excited people with their cameras waited for their turn in the downtown station. Mina was a silent pedestrian watching everything happen around her in the crowded streets.

"Hey, young lady, come here." Someone tapped her shoulder from behind and woke her from her daydreams. She turned and saw an old woman with red, curly hair and small, gray eyes. She pulled her hand away, and Mina caught the smell of sweat, cigarettes, and alcohol as she whispered in her ear, "I am Julia, but you don't have to tell me your name. You came in my dream last night—the same big brown, wild eyes, long hair, olive skin, and fit body. Yes, she is you!"

Mina stared at her. She didn't know what to say.

Julia looked at her through puffy eyes. "I knew I would see you here today," she said. She put her hand under Mina's chin and said quietly, "Give me only $20." Then Julia let go of her to bend down and search for something. Her breasts came out of her shirt like two wrinkled apples as she retrieved a piece of paper from her bra. "Blood, anger, fire, and two trees in a faraway mountainous land. Two men are all you have in your life. One man is very strong with a sword like a knight. The other is evil with black eyes and a scar on his face."

Mina froze. How could Julia know this? How could she know that the terrible man was never far from her, even on the streets of San Francisco? Mina stepped back. She felt like a seven-headed snake was trying to come out of Julia's mouth and wrap itself around Mina's throat. Her skin bristled as Julia took the last puff of her cigarette and the smoke poured from her nostrils. She threw the butt behind her and tapped Mina's chest. What she said next Mina could not decipher. She watched her purple lips move like the mouth of a dying fish.

The sky was getting dark, and her ears were freezing. She tied her green wool scarf around her neck and took out money without even counting how much it was and gave it to Julia. The crowded sidewalks, music, pets, buildings, huge orange bridge, and boats—everything was closing in on her, spinning her around like a tornado and pushing her toward a huge witch with eyes rimmed in kohl trying to swallow her.

She ran to the parking lot and spotted Erick's car with him inside it. She jumped in, breathing hard. The smell of the fast food he had bought filled the inside.

"What happened? Did you get followed by a monster?"

"I just ran away from a soothsayer."

Erick laughed, which made Mina feel better, but the things Julia said swirled around her mind, always stopping at the evil man.

The moon was full that night as it gradually rose and spread its silver color on the ocean. Small, white boats danced slowly on the blue water. It was winter, but the weather felt like spring. The milky moon balanced on the red ropes of the Golden Gate Bridge. They stood at the top of a hill, looking at the ocean behind the city. She stood so close to Erick that his jacket touched her cheek. This made her feel safe.

"I liked to watch Kandahar from the helicopter—the sky there is wonderful at night, filled with stars like diamond dust was sprayed up there. I know you miss Kandahar; so do I. It was much more than a deployment for me..." Erick's eyes turned red and sad as he looked at the ocean. The wind played with Mina's hair, and Erick put his arm around her shoulder. "Loneliness is a part of life. We came lonely into this world, and we will go out lonely someday. It is difficult, but we must be alone sometimes to find our path."

"Yes, but it is hard to pass the time alone."

Erick smiled. "But time does pass and soon it will be gone. Nothing lasts forever."

Mina looked at him. She wondered how she could feel closer to Erick than anyone in her life. He seemed to always know what she needed to hear at the right moment, as though he had grown up with her under the stars in Kandahar, as though an imaginary friend from her childhood—the one she'd spoken to on her roof at night in the summer—had come to life in America. When she was little, she had wondered if he was real, and now a quiet celestial whisper told her that he was, that it had been Erick sitting next to her counting stars all along. Her heartbeat quickened. She felt warm, she felt good; she felt like she'd finally solved the mystery of finding the one she'd always looked for.

"Are you hungry?" he asked.

Mina shook her head.

"Are you okay? You look...scared."

"I'm fine," she said. "Just a little cold."

"Here," He took off his jacket and gave it to her, "this jacket is really warm."

She marveled at him. How could he be even nicer than she'd imagined? She couldn't believe she was here, with Erick beside her, and he was real and kind, smart and good.

"What do you do when you're feeling lonely?" she asked him as they sat looking out at the ocean.

She felt like she already knew the answer, like she could see everything that came into his mind. She could tell that the water gave his body energy and his soul and mind peace.

"I find a comfort zone under the water that I can't find anywhere else. In the ocean, I am able to release whatever is bothering me." He looked at Mina. "It is a whole different world down there, where all the creatures listen to you; sometimes, you feel like it all belongs to you. From the fish who fly out of the water to the soft sands at the bottom; it is all yours. You are like a king or a queen floating through your territory. And nothing is heavy, not the air tank on your back or any of the equipment." He looked at Mina. "But when I come out of the water, the world becomes smaller again, and everything is heavy. And you must fight and swim through harsh reality all day, every day."

Mina nodded. "I've never been in the ocean like this, but I know what you are saying."

Between all words, when Erick spoke about his philosophy of life, she felt like he was speaking her own thoughts. She couldn't put the words together in English the way he did, but he was able to fill her soul with the words to describe her feelings. She couldn't explain it, but somehow, it already felt like they were one soul in two bodies.

Were these feelings there because he had appeared like an angel and saved her, temporarily at least, from a fate she was not ready to accept? No, that wasn't it. She was grateful to him, but there was something more there. She did not want to tell him how she felt, but she couldn't deny it.

Chapter 17

Hidden Shadow

*E*rick wore a black leather jacket and helmet; he held another helmet and woman's jacket in his hand.

"Let's go," he said to Mina. He got on his motorcycle, and she nervously jumped on behind him.

It was a few days before Christmas, and the streets were shining with thousands of lights blinking everywhere, even from the tree branches. The city was drowned in light. "I'm going to show you the Christmas lights from Los Altos Hills," Erick said.

She held Erick's waist on the motorcycle; this filled her with electricity. But while they rode, her mind went to the phone conversation she'd had with her parents that morning when her dad's voice had wavered. "Is he kind to you?" he had asked. "Do you like the food there? Can you ask for Naan at the market? Do you have enough money?" Her parents' questions and worries melted her heart and brought tears in her eyes. She missed them so much. She wanted to scream, to break all borders and let her parents join her and be safe for the first time in a long time. But this wasn't possible. This might never be possible. She didn't understand why the world had so many borders when they were all human; they all shared the same emotions.

The cold wind stung her face as her thoughts returned to Erick. She looked at the lights surrounding her and tried to stop her heart from the feelings that were creeping in without her permission. She had spent so much time and energy escaping from men, but escape was the last thing she wanted to do when she was with Erick. What was so different about Erick? How can I trust any man again, after everything that has happened at the hands of other men? She continued to struggle with herself as Erick stopped at a red light. He turned back to look at her and smiled. She smiled back.

After seeing the lights, Erick took her to an Afghani restaurant. He sat with his back straight at the table like a soldier. She liked his style, but never told him. Everything on the menu was familiar to her, but she wasn't hungry. She was only thinking of Erick.

Suddenly, she felt a sharp knife piercing the skin of her back. Her eyes widened, and she reached for her water glass, but the water got stuck in her throat and made her cough.

"Are you okay?" Erick said.

Haroon was sitting behind Erick, just like the hidden shadow moved with Mina. It was him; she knew it. How did he find her? She should never have left Erick's house, she told herself.

"What are you going to order? The kebab is really good," Erick said.

His face was so clear under the red restaurant lights; his scar was distinctive.

She focused on her breath as the owner of the restaurant came to their table to chat with Erick. He put his hand on Erick's shoulder and looked at Mina. "Did you bring her from Kandahar? She is pretty. You have good taste."

Erick laughed. "We are just friends, and she is my guest, old boy."

The restaurant smelled like her home. After a few minutes, the owner returned with plates of kebab and brown rice. In Dari, the owner said to Mina, "Is everything okay? You seem very tense."

She couldn't answer; Haroon was still staring at her.

He switched to English, "Erick is the best man ever, right?"

Mina forced a smile. "Yes, he is." She picked up her knife and fork and cut a piece of kebab, but it felt like a piece of rock moving between her teeth. She couldn't eat it.

She looked at the evil man behind Erick. Erick followed her eyes and turned to look at him, too. The man turned and looked out the window.

"Is something bothering you?" Erick asked.

"I...I'm not feeling so good," Mina said.

"We should go then," he said. He stood and glared at the man until he wiped his mouth and went to the restroom.

She could not talk, let alone explain to Erick what was happening. But Erick could read her eyes. He drove his bike without saying a word.

When they got home, Erick went to his room, and Mina sat on a chair in the kitchen. She noticed the green and black tea boxes Erick had bought for her. She turned on the stove to boil some water and put a tea bag in a mug for each of them, but she couldn't stop herself from looking out the window. Her heart was beating rapidly. She prayed the man would never find Erick's house.

Mina poured the boiling water into the mugs, and the smell of green tea with mint filled the kitchen. She picked up her mug and her cold fingers got warm. It felt like her blood was finally moving again.

Erick came into the living room and turned on the TV. "Do you want to watch a movie?"

She handed him a mug of tea. "Yes."

He stared at Mina's face for a few seconds and then threw the TV remote control into the opposite corner of the couch. "Forget about the movie, let's talk. Are you okay? I know you were upset before. Do you want to talk about it?"

Mina looked at him, her eyes filling. "I have terrible nightmares. I don't know when they're coming, and when they come, I don't know if they're real. I wish I could go home and escape from the nightmares, but that's where the real nightmare is. I know nobody can hurt me here. But still, I can't stop seeing him."

"Did someone hurt you in Kandahar?"

She nodded. "And now, I'm a coward. I can't go back home; I'm too scared. Every single day, one hundred times a day, I decide to leave, but the next moment, I cannot breathe or move. Why? Because I am afraid. Because being a woman in Kandahar is an endless sorrow." Her face turned red when she next looked up at him. "Maybe you need to be a woman to understand. The extremists call me a whore because I work to help women in education; they treat me like a slave and corner me with no regard for what I want. In Kandahar, they stone women who don't obey. I might be buried up to my waist with hundreds of men throwing rocks at my skull to splinter my brain. Or they'll whip me on my back and shoulders in public until I am broken. Or they'll take me as the fourth wife of an extremist man, stuck there, worrying every night if he would make love to me. They'll cut my ears and nose and kick my face if I say no to sex—or am not obedient. They'll throw acid on me and melt my skin on my way home from work. This is what awaits me if I go back to Kandahar. I physically cannot be silent in the face of extremists. If you don't want me to stay in your home, I still cannot go back; do you understand? I can't be a victim of extremism."

Her hands shook as she spoke, and after, she bit her lips. Erick hugged her without saying a word. He held her there for a few moments, then pulled her away. "I understand," he finally said. "You can stay as long as you need." He hugged her again, and she felt his heartbeat and smelled his soap. "I saw how women were treated in Kandahar; I know what you are saying. Why don't you rest now? Go to sleep and we can talk about it more tomorrow if you want, okay? Do you want some more tea or coffee? Do you want to go outside for fresh air?"

Mina shook her head. "I'm okay. I think I need to sleep. Thank you, Erick." She stood and walked to her bedroom, still biting her lips, and blaming herself for losing her temper and self-control.

Chapter 18

The Spirit of the Sequoias

The scent of the massive sequoias with their deep, red trunks filled the morning air. Mina closed her eyes and breathed the smell of wood after the rain. The car moved smoothly through the curves of the back roads, and rock music broke the silence. Red brick roofs dotted the green hills. The road got narrow and narrower as the trees became taller and wider. Mina was drowned in her thoughts until the car stopped. Erick grabbed his backpack from the backseat and gave her a bottle of water.

They scrambled up the hills with only the sound of dry leaves crunching under their feet and the song of the birds. The soil was wet from the prior night's rain. The smell of the wet soil made her soul feel alive.

Erick jumped on a giant rock in the middle of the woods. As he pulled Mina up to join him, she noticed how strong his hands were. "This is the highest point in these woods," he announced with a big smile. They sat on the huge rock like knights seizing their own territory. Mina noticed how happy he looked.

The sun warmed the rock they sat on. Once her heartbeat slowed from the climbing, she looked around at the spectrum of greens mixing with the mist from the ocean. It was as though someone had hung an amazing painting from the sky. *This is the first time I've felt this safe*, Mina thought.

"So, are you going to stay here—with me?" Erick asked as he pressed the water bottle into her hand.

She didn't answer, and Erick didn't push. He didn't need a conversation to feel comfortable. Therefore, his friends never knew what he was going to say next. His words were unpredictable. He did not ask for quick responses to his questions nor provide immediate answers.

"Don't be scared," Erick told her. "You're not home with your family, but at least you're alive, right? Just like the trees and birds around us, you are alive. And now, you can share your experience, so the world can learn from you." He leaned on the rock with his elbow. His brown eyes and hair glowed in the sunlight; the tiny, light hairs on his face were shining. He turned his glance from Mina's shoulders to the sky. "I know it is torture when we don't live where, when, and how we think we should."

Mina understood this well. They looked at the sky as the sunlight melted the wall between them. This was the wall that made their worlds so different, but it was fragile in the light.

"Look, if you want to leave, and there is a guarantee you will not die, you should go. But you know better than me what is going on over there, and it is not good. Plus, I know your family in Kandahar wants you to be safe, right? You could be safe if you stayed here with me." He tossed a small stone to the area below his feet. "I know helping educate the women in Kandahar is your destiny; that mission should belong to you—and your place is always there for you—but right now, the situation in Kandahar is not safe. It will not allow you to move toward your goals; Maybe in the future this will be possible, but not now."

Mina's body was slowly being warmed by the sun; she felt like she could even taste the light on her tongue. She looked around and felt a great connection with the woods surrounding her. She wanted to stay alive to be a part of those woods, to be one of the living creatures there, tasting life. She wanted to stay, but she was too nervous to say this to Erick. She touched the rock underneath them and felt the pulse of the redwood, the rhythmic beating of her heart, and the spirits of sequoias telling her to stay.

They looked at each other, then, but stayed silent, swirling in their thoughts and questions. Mina's heart was on the verge of exploding by being with Erick, but her eastern prudency didn't let her talk about her feelings. She didn't even know what to call this feeling—love? She couldn't have been next to Erick and not be in love. Couldn't be beside him and not see the world more beautiful. But she couldn't resist all the stubborn feelings that pushed her back, telling her being in love doesn't matter; staying in love matters.

Erick took his camera out of his backpack and set it up facing the valley and tall sequoia trees. The camera flashed. Erick adjusted the lens, hesitantly threw his hand around Mina's arm, smiled, and pressed the button. Mina's eyes were into a large red butterfly that was fluttering into the bushes. Oh, how eager she was for that moment and Erick's hearty smile. At the most pleasant instant, their first photo snapped.

As Erick was rolling the camera around in his hands and playing with its lens, he said, "Do you know, for a while I have wanted to walk with you at night under the moonlight, by the beach, or in the secluded alleys?" He squeezed Mina's arm and said, "Don't be afraid; no one here will ask about our relationship." Mina laughed and Erick said, "One of these nights, you and I will walk under the moonlight." He placed his camera in backpack, jumped off the rock, and raised his hand to help Mina. There was a flowing energy around them that brought them closer to each other unconsciously.

The smell of hot milk, cocoa, sugar, chocolate, fresh cake, and coffee filled the small shop cottage. It smelled like their home on Eid Nowruz nights when Mother scrupulously molded all the sweets in the oven on the Eve of Eid and Mina sprayed coconut powder on them.

A small, wooden round table with two large chairs next to the coffee shop window invited them to pure privacy.

Erick came with two large cups and said, "Got your coffee with vanilla flavor. Do you like it? Vanilla is my favorite." He moved his chair close to Mina's so that there was no distance between them. Both were sitting close together in front of the large window. Only the green hill in front of them was looking at them stealthily. The bitter aroma of Erick's coffee came from his mouth and hit Mina's face. It was like a sweet breeze. It was a lovely perfume to her.

Erick's fingertips, warmed by the glass, moved on Mina's hands, squeezed both, and he said, "For a while, I have wanted to tell you to live a little and let go of all the sorrow of your country. Your compassionate attitude towards your people and your hometown is admirable, but don't you think you should escape this grief for a while? Sorrow is just like the swamp—it drags us deeper and deeper day by day if we don't escape from it. It won't go by itself. We need to escape from sorrow. Listen, we are the same age, and when they shaped these wars in Afghanistan, we were not yet born. I came to your hometown to defend my homeland and keep the peace, and you did your best to help your people and build your community. We both fulfilled our civil commitment to our countries and our people, but whatever policy has been behind this war no longer pertains to us. Whatever happens, it is not your responsibility. War and peace have always been an integral part of humanity, and it will continue to be after us. Therefore, live a little!"

"Straight out, it's hard to have feelings about someone, but I've been through all this hardship for you. Because your infinite and sincere goodness have made all the impossible possible. And I feel, somehow, you have the same feelings.

"You might say that this is not a good time to talk about feelings. Well, you are right. You are dealing with a lot of things now. But you can handle all these things *and* experience life *and* give the feelings a chance." The warmth of Erick's hands, and his words, engulfed Mina. She was thirsty to hear these words from him.

Erick hit Mina's knee, "And you will not be harmed by me because you have opened a special place in my heart. A space as wide as the sky.

"Believe me, when I am with you, it makes the world meaningful to me, even with all its inequality and cruelty. Look, I'm not a man of beautiful words, especially when it comes to talking about feelings. I become speechless; I don't even know how all these words came out of my mouth today," He blushed. "I've seen so many movies, read many books, and know many women and men wounded by love. But just telling you one sentence like, 'I'm not the kind of man that would hurt a woman,' is difficult.

"If sometimes you see me dipping out on my own, preferring silence and isolation over everything, it doesn't mean I don't like being with you. Sometimes I need to take a place under the cold rocks, just like a crab, to get energized and go back to the pond." He squeezed Mina's hands harder. "You are the lady of Kandahar, and you have a heart as vast and beautiful as the star-filled Kandahar sky. You know what I'm saying?"

Mina's heart melted by those words that touched her heart deeply. Her eyes became watery and said, "I believe love is not like a bird—throwing it in a cage and enjoying its voice in the corner of the house. So, we can love each other infinitely and even live far apart. Or can be extremely in love—and there is no captivity for love. Right?"

Erick smiled. "Yes, and there is no power in the world to stop us from the things we really want to do." He blinked. "Nobody can jail your free, wild feminine, elegant, fancy soul!" Then, they both laughed loudly.

They left their coffee on the table. Mina got up to take her handbag from the arm of the chair and was surprised by Erick's unpredictable kiss on her forehead, a kiss that gave Mina a sense of affection, security, and protection. It was like Erick had kissed her soul. And she had such a heartfelt experience that it seemed like the kiss was healing of all the pain of her past. They hugged each other while only a breath was between them.

Chapter 19

Permanent Nightmares

Mina heard a whining sound. She woke up suddenly and turned on the lamp on the nightstand. She stood and tiptoed outside the door of Erick's room. She wanted to knock, but instead, she stopped and stood in front of it.

She remembered a summer Kandahar night when she was sleepless from the heat and left her bedroom to sleep on a wooden bench in the middle of the yard. She saw a woman with long, black hair to her waist and a long, white dress come out from the basement and sit right above her head. No, Mina wasn't afraid. She just gazed at the lady's beautiful hands that were shining under the moonlight, and then she disappeared in the blink of an eye. Sometimes she saw a creature with hooves of an animal and head of a human coming out of the basement making an anomalous sound, but it disappeared in a second. She heard strange noises that were far from reality. All those things were not scary to her at all. She told herself that a house two centuries old must have many secrets. Perhaps that's why her grandmother put scissors under her pillow every night and prayed on four sides of her bedroom and band bad spirits with prayers. But one night she saw that hoof animal with the face of Haroon. He was standing beside her bed. She attacked Haroon with grandma's scissors from under her pillow. She was woken up by her screaming. Oh, how scared was that cold winter nightmare and now the same horrors moved under her skin slowly just behind Erick's bedroom door.

Erick looked up and saw his friend's dead body, naked. He was attached to a tree by two ropes; nothing but the grey sky filled the space above his face. His belt was wound around his mouth, his hands tied together by one of the ropes. His uniform, rank, medals, hat, boots, gun, and even his bag, hung from different branches of the same tree. The branches cracked as they swayed in the wind. The roaring sands of Kandahar blew through his skull. Fire was sparking in front of him; two men covered in gray shawls held the end of an iron pole in the fire and watched it turn red. Everywhere was silent, and Erick felt like he was in a gap between the reality in front of him and the reality of his bedroom far away. The men picked up the molten hot stick and held it to his chest. Erick could smell the burning hair and skin. His friend. A strong pain filled his heart. He bit his tongue hard and tasted the salty blood.

He screamed and twisted in pain. "Give me your gun!" Erick begged the men. One of those men put a Colt in Erick's outstretched hand. The two men laughed. He put the Colt to his temple...

He opened his eyes and looked down at his own bed. He was sweating badly, and his insides were burning. He opened the small drawer of his nightstand and pulled out the Colt Commander.

He looked at it for a while, not blinking. His hands were shaking. He was going to do it; would he pull the trigger this time?

He heard a knock at his door. He did not turn his face or turn on the light.

"Are you in there, Erick? I heard a noise. Can you please come and check around the house with me?"

When he heard Mina's voice, his eyes blinked open. His hands shuddered when he looked down and saw the gun. He'd had this kind of nightmare ever since returning from Kandahar, but this one was so real it broke the border between nightmare and real life.

He breathed in, collecting his broken pieces, and grafting them. "I'm okay, Mina. You should go to sleep. It was me you heard; I think I had a nightmare. Sorry if I woke you up."

His Kandahar wound was not healed; he could not find any treatment for it. He hadn't wanted to talk about it with anyone. He didn't want anyone to know how broken he was, how bad his nightmares were. He didn't think anyone understood.

He opened his bedroom window and the cold, fresh air hit his naked body.

His back shivered, but he did not close the window. He needed the air. *No one could understand how this feels*, he thought. *I am not created to be with anyone.* He breathed rapidly and tried to forget about the feelings he had been denying for Mina. But he asked himself, what if Mina hadn't knocked on his door and called to him? Would he still be alive? He put his pillow over his face and thought how easily death could happen to him. Somehow, he had escaped it before. But even though he hadn't died, he also hadn't really been alive since coming home, and he wasn't sure he ever could be again.

The next day, sunlight reflected on his body through the palm fronds. He put his palms on the grass and pushed his body up and down. The veins pushed out from the skin of his arms like ropes twisting and pulling underneath. After a while, he sat on a bench, breathing fast. He dropped his white towel around his neck and drank a whole bottle of water. He was starting to feel better about the nightmare from the night before. He still had a little headache, but he was used to that. The headaches were part of his life.

Mina watched him from the kitchen window for a while and then looked away. She was surprised when he walked up right behind her.

"Did I scare you?" he asked when he saw her startle. He reached around her to fill the coffee maker with tap water.

"No, not at all," she said, then smiled and looked at the tattoos on his back. "Did you know that tattoos are like a book?"

"What do you mean?"

"They tell me a story, the story of you."

Erick laughed loudly. "I see! So, while I was working out, you were exploring me like a lab rat to read my story?"

She laughed. "Not a rat—more like a strong, masculine lion. But did you know Kandahar's gypsies have many tattoos? They speak to each other through their tattoos. Kandahar's gypsy women even tattoo their face, chin, forehead, and hands."

"See! Gypsy women speak more easily than you; they tell stories with their whole body." They both laughed

Erick stood in front of the mirror in his bathroom, running the electric razor over his cheeks and chin. He crumpled his tongue inside his mouth to shave better. When he turned off the razor, he applied aftershave and made his face skin sting.

He saw Mina walk by several times, checking out the rooms, doors, and windows. She walked around the pool and even looked behind the trees in the backyard. She did this every night. One time, she asked him to show her the door to the basement. But Erick never told her where it was because it was hidden under her bed in the guest room. He hadn't known why she always seemed worried before, but now he understood.

"I'll be back a little later," he said before he left the house. He needed to think.

When he got home, a fragrant smoke filled the house. When it cleared up a little, he saw a feast on the table. Mina pushed the oven door closed with her leg; her hands full of brightly-colored dishes filled with food. Succulent smells filled his nose.

"I'm starving!" he said, and he dropped his car keys on the corner of the table and sat without changing his clothes.

"Good!" Mina said and squeezed a glass of ice water for Erick in between two plates.

While Erick ate, she watched him to see if he looked happy. When he was too full to eat any more, Mina asked, "Which one did you like? Spicy chicken? Saffron rice? Kebab?

Erick smiled. "All of it. Did you cook all day?"

She shrugged her shoulders. She had barely eaten anything.

Erick sipped his drink and looked at her. "Can I ask you a question?" he said.

Mina nodded.

"I don't want to make you uncomfortable, but I want to make sure you feel safe in my home."

She paused. "I do feel comfortable." She wanted to tell him more, but she stopped herself. She walked to the couch in the living room and sat down.

"Good," he said, sensing there was something more but not wanting to push. He looked away. "Do you want to go out then?"

"Tonight?" she asked. "Isn't it cold outside?"

He sat on the arm of the blue couch. "Are you scared to leave and come back? Or do you just not want to go out with me?"

Mina looked down at her lap; her hair covered half of her face. There were so many things she wanted to say, but she didn't know where to begin. Her face turned red. The clock on the wall struck ten times.

Finally, Erick broke the silence. "Nobody can hurt you in this house; no one can even touch you in this city! But whatever is bothering you, if you don't want to talk about it, it's okay."

He stood up from the arm of the couch, but Mina grabbed his hand before he could walk away.

Her chin trembled. "There is a man who follows me. Have you seen him? His eyes are darkened; his name is Haroon."

"No, I haven't seen him. Are you sure he followed you here? Who is he? What did he do to you?" Erick grabbed her hand in his.

Mina told him her story. "That afternoon, the sky was gray. Wind hit the doors and windows, rattling them. I was very nervous; the wind ignited my worries like fire. My father was traveling, and my mom was not home. I was looking at the washed clothes hanging on the line in the yard. I sensed there was a reason behind the wind's howl. Suddenly, the sky turned red, so I wound my scarf around my face and began to grab the clothes from the line to bring them inside. The sand hit my eyes like needles. More and more sand came. I was fighting the wind and sand to save the clothes, but suddenly, I felt a rough hand on my back. Another hand reached around to cover my mouth. I turned and threw the clothes at the man, then punched him, but he pushed me into the corner. I knew he was from the Taliban because of his eyes. A deep scar cut his lips and chin and across his cheek. I couldn't yell, only punch at his chest. He pulled me to the corner of the yard. The sandstorm made everything blurry, and his hands pressed harder against my mouth.

'Shut up! Shut up!' he said, repeatedly.

"I wanted to bite his hands, but I could not move. My body was thin, not strong enough to push him back. He grabbed my hair and hit my head on the cement wall of the yard. My shirt tore, and I felt a heavy body on me. Warm blood seeped from my head onto my back. I could not breathe; I felt empty, mashed, dizzy. Melted, destroyed, shattered. I vomited, but still I could not see or hear; I could only smell a putrid body on me and feel the sharp pain between my legs that filled my whole body.

"When he left, I wanted to get up, but I did not have enough energy to move. It was like I was weighed down by heavy chains. My body was like a mummy coming out from a dark and deep grave after a thousand years with no blood. My bones felt like they were tied together with rough ropes. I went to my room, pulled my hands free from the mummy's ropes, and closed the curtains. I saw the backyard through the window turn into nonsensical geometric shapes that rolled on each other.

"I felt like I had just come from an unknown land and a different dimension, a place where I could not feel anything except millions of tiny, blackened eyes hanging from me, chewing my body little by little."

Erick swallowed. After a few moments, he said, "Haroon did this to you? And this has been your nightmare ever since?"

Mina nodded.

"And you've never told anyone?

"It was not a good idea to talk about it with anybody; most people there would see me as a sinner rather than a victim, and I didn't feel comfortable enough to tell my family either. You're the first person I've told. I try to forget what happened, to forget everything, but I can't do it, Erick. It is hooked in my brain forever. My family thought he was only a burglar from the Taliban who came into our home; they didn't want to know the truth, and I didn't want to tell them. I was only fourteen! Now this man has friends in the government, so he thinks he can have me by force. And he watches me to make sure I don't tell anyone what he did.

He is older now; he doesn't want to lose his high position or his money."

She looked at him through tear-filled eyes. But even as she cried, when she breathed in, she felt the air moving easily through her throat. A heavy stone had fallen from her shoulders. It was like a bird had been released from a sticky and dark cage after many years. She felt exhausted but free.

Erick grabbed her cold hands in his. "I'm so sorry, Mina. Your nightmare is different than mine, but I know how it feels."

She put her head on his shoulder. The smell of him made her feel so safe and secure, like dry land soaked by rain after many years of drought. Erick's hands combed through her hair, and his warm breath touched her earlobe. When she looked up, he noticed her face looked brighter, like a mask of sadness had been removed. Erick saw beauty in her he hadn't seen before. Before long, she stood and went to her room without checking the doors, windows, or backyard.

Erick felt weak compared to Mina. He went to the backyard, turned off the lights and walked in circles in the dark. He looked at the sky. Twinkling stars shone above the palm trees. If he listened hard enough, he could still hear the roaring sands of Kandahar. It was as though he had brought tinnitus from Kandahar that would stay with him forever, reminding him of the day his friend died. The sound stayed with him, but the voice of his heart spoke louder and deeper.

He did not know how his story and Mina's were connected. He was a very logical man; he evaluated everything he did. But that night, his logic was like two scorpions fighting, biting each other, like his emotions. He had not cried when he lost his friend in Kandahar. But on this night, he was so angry, he cried and pounded the punching bag on his patio for hours. He hit it rapidly as he thought about the war in Kandahar, all the difficulties, and the burned body of his friend.

He stopped when there was pain in his wrist. His shirt was drenched in sweat; he took it off to wipe his tears and his body. He had finally shed tears for the Kandahar wounds they had both held quietly for years and the invisible wounds that Kandahar women could not talk about. The tears he was finally able to shed polished his soul and his mind.

He took a cold shower, but still he was burning on the inside. He opened the small window of his bathroom. Cold night air rushed in, but he still burned.

He went to his room to lie on his bed, but he knew he couldn't sleep. He turned on his laptop and clicked on his Kandahar trip pictures. He looked at the pictures from the helicopter and remembered the day he arrested men from the Taliban in Maiwand. He had blindfolded them and handcuffed them to the back of the inside of his helicopter, but he had wanted revenge. He wanted to kick out the insurgents from his helicopter and break their necks, but he didn't do that.

He rolled over and thought about Mina. She had come into his home, mind, and spirit, and he wanted to protect her from all the bitter and unfortunate parts of life. Finally, his eyes got tired.

Chapter 20

The Endless Blue

It was Sunday morning. He had tossed and turned in his bed all night, his mind filled with painful memories and lifelong struggles, but the enigmatic feelings he usually woke with were gone.

Erick opened the window from his bed and looked at the foggy morning sky. It did not feel heavy like a gravestone on his chest. He noticed the sensation of blood moving slowly through his vessels and his heart beating regularly. He put his hands on his chest and felt the strong beat with his palm. Even though he had woken in this same room every day for many years, he felt like a new world was opening to him, and he wasn't sure why.

New feelings were growing in him that he couldn't explain. He looked in the backyard and saw Mina feeding his dog. The dog was sitting close to her, wagging his tail rapidly. He looked at his dog like he was seeing him for the first time.

He felt lucky for everything surrounding him. He looked at Mina again, and unknown feelings filled him in waves. He hadn't thought about her in this way before. How could he have feelings for her, now? She was so vulnerable and scared. Did this make him a bad person? Maybe, he was confusing the ability to feel again with an appreciation for the person who had brought him back to life. He could not trust these feelings. He pushed them away like a cloud blocking the sun.

He did not want to talk to Mina until he understood the motivation and truth behind his feelings. All Sunday, he busied himself planting flowers in his garden. He replaced the garden soil, then cleaned up the dry leaves and pruned branches of the trees. He put some flowers in a vase for the table. When was the last time he had done that? He wasn't sure. He swept the dirt from the pool deck and scrubbed the mud off his hands and knees. At one point, he stopped and put his muddy hand on his chest. It still felt fresh and new and strong, and the feelings in his heart remained. He was so happy to feel again.

Mina told herself she should leave the house and walk around the block. *I must go home*, she thought. *I miss my family.* She thought of the last hug from her dad before she left. His shoulders had shivered before he said goodbye to her. *It doesn't matter what fate awaits me. I must go because Haroon will insult my father if he finds out that I'm living in the house of a US military man...but not an insult greater than what he did to me.*

Erick had awakened feelings in her she didn't think she could have after everything that had happened. He was not like any man she had met before. He said she could stay, but did she want to? Not just for survival, but for him? She was afraid to lose herself in her feelings for him and didn't want her feelings to impact her decision to stay or go.

She walked the neighborhood for hours and hours; it was almost afternoon when she sat on a small wooden bench in the corner of the park. She sat there and cried for an hour until there were no more tears to shed. The weather was cloudy and windy, but since it was early spring, the trees had begun to bloom, and the blossoms were falling from the branches onto Mina's shoulders and hair.

Her eyes were on the cherry tree while a small finch fell from the branches on her lap. She picked up the little, poor bird that was shaking and small. Its blue tail shivered rapidly. Mina said, "You know little bird, I am scared and tired just like you. And if I rest my whole life and swallow all the sedative pills in the world, I would still be tired. Where did you come from? I come from war. I have fought for a long time to survive. I still survived with undetonated mines in my homeland—with grenades separated from toggles around my house—bullets left in the guns in my land. See! I survived. You will survive too, but you will be full of memories!" She rubbed the warm bird's body to her cheeks. "What a surprise you came to me. I'm usually afraid of being surprised. Do you know what? When the mines exploded under the feet of the children in my homeland, when the skin and hair, dolls and toys, all burned in the fire—those burnt, dark little bodies were burnt in my mind forever.

Oh, my little bird, I'm afraid that a young man from my neighboring country, with long, curly hair and a beard that has just grown on his face, hid his dreams inside a suicide vest and came to my homeland for Jehad and blew himself up in our alley to see the seventy beautiful virgin women of paradise who have been promised to him. He tore himself and others into thousands of pieces. My beloved bird, remember that there is neither heaven nor hell if you and I do not exist in this world. Even Moses could not hit his magic wand into the blood river of Afghanistan to dry it. Jesus cannot heal those blind Taliban with their explosive vests, and Mohammad wondered why people blew themselves up in his name.

My lovely bird, all of them spoke about love and a God who bathes all of us with the water of love instead of the human blood. But those extremists sold their soul to Satan for a new religion under an explosive suicide vest." The birds stopped shivering and looked like it came down on Mina's hands just to listen to her; its tiny red eyes didn't even blink.

"Did you know I am not scared of the possibility of a meteor hitting the Earth—from earthquakes, storms, volcanoes, and a thousand other natural disasters? I am afraid of endless war in my land and the guns on the streets of Kandahar targeting my head. I am afraid of fire in Kandahar's roofed bazaar when those men with suicide vests are hidden around and blow themselves up while women shopping for new clothes and jewelry for Eid. Yes, my little bird, that is my fear: women's gold bracelets and necklaces clinging to their skin and melting in the fire, the colorful clothes hanging from the shops are turning into ashes, burned women and kids' bodies being engulfed in a tunnel of fire and blood. My little bird, even if the explosions stop in Kandahar, how can I get along with Talibs? They don't look at me as a woman; they look at me as a weak creature that doesn't even exist!

You go to your own home now, my little bird; you will be safe. I won't get back home, and I won't be safe. I am a woman, and my home does not belong to women anymore."

She kissed its soft blue and yellow feathers and left it under the tree carefully. She said, "You can tell your children tonight that love does what people cannot do. If those people tasted love a little bit, they would never start wars."

She felt cold and wiped her watery eyes with her scarf. It was time to go back to Erick's.

Later in the afternoon, Erick washed his hands with the hose and went inside. Mina was sitting at his computer desk in the living room. Her hair was wet from a recent shower; the fragrance of her shampoo wafted into his nose.

He looked at her back for a while, then finally said, "Do you want to go watch the sunset?"

She turned from the computer and looked at him. "I'd love to."

He went into his room and came out wearing dark jeans and a navy-blue, collared shirt that made his skin glow. His eyes were shining and bright where there usually was sadness. He walked to the kitchen, grabbed the dog food from the pantry, and filled the bowl. When he petted him, the big brown dog barked loudly. It seemed like he, too, noticed a difference.

Mina chose sandals and a sleeveless floral dress Rebecca had picked out for her in Washington D.C. She had never worn this type of American dress before; her body was not hidden like it usually was. As Erick watched her step into the front yard, she enjoyed how it felt to be in something that fit. She liked not feeling ashamed of her curves. She was feminine, and she was beautiful. Her long, straight hair flowed past her shoulders, and her eyes sparkled with happiness.

Erick's hands held the steering wheel, and Mina sat next to him. So much had changed that neither of them knew what to say. Silence is God's language, Mina thought. Erick noticed it, too. He did not want to break the mysterious and sweet silence and replace it with dry words that could never capture how he felt.

The car moved smoothly along the coast. Erick had driven this way a thousand times at least, but this time, everything felt new. The flowers, trees, and grass—even the ocean felt aromatic and fresh.

They were late. The sun had set on the endless, blue ocean and only a dark orange color lit the horizon and reflected on the sand.

They looked at each other and walked to the cliff. Erick stood behind Mina and wrapped his arms around her. He embraced a world full of hope and harmony, and Mina felt like the world was assuming an organized shape with everything exactly where it belonged. She was a tiny piece of a large universe. Her feelings moved with the wind and clouds, the moon and water, the fish, shells, and coral. The soft sand under her feet would lead her wherever she needed to be. The earth had magnetized her body and soul. Her hands felt warm and comfortable under his. For today, she belonged here, with Erick.

"To me, a sunset is a symbol of the cycle of the sun. Next, it will rise again, day after day, year after year, century after century. No matter where we are, sunsets remind me that life is continuing," Erick said.

Mina felt so close to him. She turned and put her head on his strong chest. Mina pulled her hair behind her ear, looked into his eyes, and smiled. Erick's hands wove into her hair, and his warm breath hit her face and melted her inside. Mina felt like she was in a different dimension where time and place were meaningless. She was alive at that moment, not drowning in the past, not dreading the future. Just being there, with him. The crashing waves mixed with the sound of Erick's heartbeat and made the best symphony she had ever heard.

They came down from the cliff and took off their shoes. Their feet sank into the soft sand of Half Moon Bay as rain drops slowly started to fall. The ocean was roaring, and the clouds thundered. The rain felt warm on their faces as they looked at each other.

Erick grabbed her hands and smiled. "Rain is always a good sign, isn't it?" Mina laughed and nodded. It felt like they tasted life for the first time when wild warm kisses rose between them like two sea birds flying, slowly joining with the rain, clouds, waves, and sky.

Farzana Ebrahimi
December 2020

About The Author

Farzana Ebrahimi was born July, 1981 in Kandahar, Afghanistan to an educated and opened-mind family. Her mother was a teacher and her father a hydraulic engineer. Farzana founded Kandahar's Health and Development Organization to support women in Kandahar when she was only 24 years old. She trained hundreds of women in educational projects after the Taliban was removed from Afghanistan from 2001-2010. Farzana worked over a decade for gender equality and was a women's rights activist in Kandahar. She moved to northern California in 2010 and continued to support Afghan women from there. Farzana Ebrahimi was the woman of the month in June 2010 as a remarkable woman in Lifetime TV in America because of her efforts for Afghan women's rights.

Gender equality was her passion when she was only 8 years old. Farzana took off her hijab in the middle of a hot summer in Kandahar and ran from school to home. While winds touched her hair, she asked herself why she needed to wear a Hijab, while boys did not? In the closed society of Kandahar her ideas were rejected. She believed in women's rights and wanted to bring change for women in Kandahar and continued her path. Farzana received an honorable bachelor's degree in leadership from Northwood University of Texas. Farzana has loved writing since childhood and spent long years indoors writing about all the events in Kandahar. She was jailed at home as a teenage girl by the Taliban from 1996-2001. Farzana Ebrahimi began her professional writing career when she moved in California.

Index

1-Arghandab is a river in Afghanistan, about 400 km in length near the city of Kandahar.

2-Baba Wali is a Sufi saint. Many people trek to his mausoleum in Kandahar to pay homage to him. Women can only enter on Wednesdays.

3-Elephant Mountain is one of the mysterious and spectacular mountains of Kandahar.

4-Harmala is a seed that is used traditionally in the Middle East as a disinfectant and air purifier and best of luck.

5-Mulla is a term that is sometimes used for a man who has a higher education in Islamic theology and sacred law.

6-Naan is a leavened, oven-baked flatbread found in Afghanistan

7-Perhan Turban is the traditional clothing worn by men in Afghanistan

8-Qabeli Palaw is a traditional famous Afghan food. It consists of steamed rice mixed with raisins.

9-Registan is a sandy desert consisting of small, red, sand hills located in Kandahar.

10-Sharia courts are where people are tried for crimes against the traditional religious Sharia law.

CPSIA information can be obtained
at www.ICGtesting.com
Printed in the USA
LVHW012312300122
709721LV00003B/249

9 781951 451097